BAD SAMARITAN

BAD SAMARITAN

LUCAS STONE
BOOK 2

MARK ALLEN

WOLFPACK PUBLISHING
— EST 2013 —

Bad Samaritan
Paperback Edition
Copyright © 2023 Mark Allen

Wolfpack Publishing
9850 S. Maryland Parkway, Suite A-5 #323
Las Vegas, Nevada 89183

wolfpackpublishing.com

Paperback ISBN 978-1-63977-968-0
eBook ISBN 978-1-63977-967-3
LCCN 2022951620

"Evil people always support each other; that is their chief strength."

ALEXANDER SOLZHENITSYN

ONE

"HE'S ON THE RUN, sheriff! Moving like a damn jackrabbit!"

"Got it." Lucas Stone ended the call on his cellphone and tossed it onto the passenger seat of his 1978 Chevy Blazer. Through the windshield, he spotted a slim figure dressed in black burst from the alleyway behind the used bookstore and sprint into the road right in front of him.

Stone slammed the brakes and skidded to a stop, narrowly missing the runner before he disappeared into the shadows of the nearest backyard. Had he been a murder suspect or something like that, Stone probably would have just gunned it and turned him into roadkill. But he didn't reckon shoplifting deserved a death sentence.

He grabbed the microphone from its cradle. "Valentine, this is Stone. Got a runner, wearing all black. Ducked into a backyard on Olive Street, heading north."

There came a burst of radio static, followed by the voice of Cade Valentine, the youngest deputy in the department. "10-4, sheriff. I'm down by the middle school, just past the greenhouse. I'll head that way, come in from the other end and try to cut him off."

As Stone exited the truck, he heard Valentine's sirens wail to life less than a mile away, just over the hill. Satisfied that backup was coming, he yanked his keys from the ignition and took off after the thief. His footsteps pounded on the pavement, sounding like drumbeats in the night.

Whisper Falls was too small for a Walmart but Jeremy Sloane had studied the giant corporation carefully, then opened his own small-town version of a modern general store complete with a pharmacy and sandwich shop. Scrupulous organizational skills and meticulous record-keeping kept Sloane's Emporium ticking like a clock. The place featured most of the same items you'd find at the big box stores in Milford, Malone, or Plattsburgh.

Unfortunately, all that stuff served as targets for shoplifters. To combat the thievery, Sloane had hired Tom 'Raff' Rafferty, one of the best loss-prevention specialists in the tri-lakes region. Raff was very good at his job and Stone respected him, so he had been happy to help when the call came through.

Stone spotted the shoplifter up ahead, wearing a backpack as he crossed one backyard and clambered over the fence to the next. Stone poured on some speed and closed the gap. He stretched out his hand to grab a scrap of the black hoodie. He missed, just a half second too late.

He snarled a curse that would have been wildly inappropriate had he been standing behind the pulpit on Sunday morning. No doubt about it, this son of a bitch was fast. Or maybe Stone was just getting old.

Screw that.

He vaulted over the fence in hot pursuit.

Valentine's siren screamed like a banshee in the night, closing in fast. The thief careened out into the yard with his backpack flapping and dashed out onto the street. Stone circled around to the other side of the house, looking to cut him off.

He moved to intercept, reaching out to put hands on the guy, but the thief proved fast and slippery. He twisted away from Stone's grasp, backpedaled, and switched direction. He slipped on a muddy patch of lawn but managed to stay upright and dart away again.

Stone took up the chase again, teeth gritted, legs pumping, just two steps behind. He could feel the burn in his muscles but it was mostly neutralized by the adrenaline coursing through him.

Valentine's squad car appeared at the end of the street, fishtailing around the corner. Emergency lights strobed the night as the thief seemed to flag. Probably realized that with two cops running him down, there was no way out.

Valentine's cruiser skidded to a stop and the deputy emerged with his gun drawn.

"Hold it right there!" Valentine leveled the pistol. Even from twenty yards away, Stone could see the muzzle shaking. Being a rookie, this was probably the first time Valentine had pulled his pistol in the line of duty.

The thief spun on his heel and tried to flee in the opposite direction, down a dead end street. But he had hesitated too long.

Stone closed the gap and collided with the guy in a takedown tackle. The air exploded from the perp's lungs as the blow knocked him down onto the pavement, Stone's crushing weight on top of him. Valentine appeared a moment later, this time holding handcuffs instead of his Glock.

The cuffs clicked into place. "Got him!"

Stone stood up and used his boot to roll the guy over.

His eyes narrowed when he recognized the man. "Scooby," he growled. "What the hell?" Stone reached down, grabbed a handful of hoodie, and yanked the thief to his feet.

'Scooby' Taylor was a local meth-head and small-time crook. His bloodshot eyes were watery and an untidy mop of red curls leaked out from under his wool cap. He wore a ragged coat that looked like it had suffered a moth feeding frenzy. His pants had so many tears in them that his legs had to be freezing from the November cold. Late autumn in the Adirondack Mountains was not conducive to exposed skin.

When Scooby opened his mouth to speak, Stone saw the rotted stumps of his teeth and caught a whiff of breath that smelled like a dead skunk's asshole.

"I ain't got nothing!" Scooby twisted and tried to pull away from Valentine's grip. "I ain't resisting and I ain't boosting and I ain't got nothing! And I wasn't running!"

Stone wanted to pop him in the mouth just to shut him up. But he managed to resist the urge and said, "Take a breath and relax."

"Relax? That's your advice? Easy for you to say. You're not the one all trussed up like a hog for the slaughterhouse."

"It's just a pair of handcuffs," said Valentine. "Not like I slapped leg irons on you."

"Not yet, anyway," Scooby retorted with a glare. "But give it time. I know how you badge boys work."

"Shut up, Scooby." Stone grabbed the backpack. "Let's see what you've got in here."

"Hey!" Scooby yelled belligerently. "You can't do that without a warrant!"

"That right?" Stone unzipped the bag and started rooting around inside.

"Yeah, that's right! And you can't handcuff me

either!" Scooby twisted against his restraints again. "I'm not any danger to you."

"You feeling okay?" Stone asked.

"Yeah. Why?"

"Because you've got enough cough syrup in here to knock out a buffalo." Stone pulled out a bottle of night-time cold medicine. "What do you need eleven of these for?"

Scooby opened his mouth, reconsidered, and slammed it shut again.

"Can't hear you," Stone said.

Scooby's eyes flicked around in their sockets like a cornered animal. "I ain't got nothing to say."

"I think you've got plenty to say." Stone settled his honey-colored eyes on the thief. "This shit contains ephedrine, and you stole more than enough for someone to cook up a nice batch of crank."

Scooby exercised his right to remain silent.

"Can't be you," Stone said. "Takes smarts and God left those out when He put you together."

"Kiss my sweaty ass-crack, copper."

"That's just being rude." Stone shoved Scooby toward Valentine's patrol car. "You're under arrest. We'll continue this chat down at the station. Maybe sitting in a cell for a few hours will do you some good."

"Wait," Scooby said. "I just remembered something."

"What?"

Scooby grinned slyly at Stone with his blackened teeth stumps. "I remembered that I want a damn lawyer."

"And I remembered that I want to punch you in the mouth," Stone replied. "We'll see which one you get first."

Stone had only been sheriff for ten months but that was plenty long enough for him to realize that Garrison County—hell, the entire northern region of the Adirondack Mountains—had a methamphetamine problem. Maybe not yet plague levels but definitely a malignant cancer that needed to be eradicated.

It had even crept into his church, the devil's poison infiltrating sacred ground. In addition to his sheriff position, Stone was also the pastor of Faith Bible Church in Whisper Falls. Attendance had grown since he took over due to his earthy, no-bullshit style of preaching, and he had seen the signs of meth usage creeping through the fringes of his congregation. The signs were subtle but they were there.

Yeah, it was a cancer and it needed to be burned out before it spread further and destroyed more lives.

"He's still demanding to see his lawyer," Valentine said as he and Stone stared through the two-way mirror into the interview room where Scooby sat alone at the table, picking at the dirt under his fingernails.

Stone sipped some coffee to knock the chill from his bones, letting the heat seep through him. Early November wasn't exactly tropical up here in the Adirondacks, though it was nothing compared to the sub-zero temperatures that would deliver an arctic blast in January and February. "Who'd he call?"

"Slidell." Valentine sounded disgusted, as if just saying the name left his tongue slathered in dog shit.

Stone sighed and glanced at his watch. If Scooby had called Scott Slidell, it wouldn't be long before Garrison County's foremost ambulance chaser arrived at the station to bail his client out of jail. The defense attorney prided himself on being a stumbling block for cops and seemed to appear like magic whenever a scumbag got arrested. He also happened to be a pompous prick.

"I'm going to take another crack at Scooby." Stone put down his coffee cup.

"That legal? He's lawyered up."

"Not exactly."

Valentine shrugged. "You're the boss."

"Just let me know when Slidell shows up."

"Will do."

Stone walked into the interview room. Scooby had stopped fidgeting with his fingernails and now just sat there with his head bowed, motionless. He looked more like a wax museum dummy than an actual human being.

"Let's talk, Scooby." Stone leaned against the wall and crossed his arms. "You got your phone call, right?"

Scooby's eyes shifted to glance at Stone, but that was his only movement. His mouth stayed firmly shut.

"Just so you know, Slidell's on his way."

Scooby perked up slightly at this news.

"I'm sure you'll be out on bail in no time, but maybe there's a better deal on the table."

Scooby broke his silence to ask, "Yeah? Like what?"

"I can drop the theft charges if you tell me who's cooking meth around here."

"No way." Scooby shook his head and frowned. "Ain't happening."

"Once meth gets into a town, things go to hell fast," Stone said. "This isn't a game. You need to tell me who's cooking."

"I don't need to tell you jack-all," Scooby sneered. "What're you gonna do, beat me 'til I talk? Trust me, the people I work for will do a whole lot worse than that to me if I tell you anything."

"What people?"

Before Scooby could answer—not that he was going to anyway—there was a knock on the door. Valentine poked his head in, looking worried. "Sorry, sheriff, but you've got a phone call."

"Tell them to leave a message."

"I think you should take this one, sir."

The deputy's firm tone more than his actual words convinced Stone that he should take the call. He pushed away from the wall and stepped out of the interview room, closing the door behind him.

"This better not be Slidell jerking my chain," he said.

"It's not Slidell. I wouldn't have bothered you for that moron." Valentine handed him a cellphone. "It's the fire marshal. Said he needs to talk to you and said it was urgent, even after I told him you were in the middle of an interrogation."

Puzzled, Stone held the phone up to his ear. "Stone here."

"Sheriff, this is Dennis Fox."

Fox was the Garrison County Fire Marshal. He and Stone had met in passing a few times but weren't that well acquainted. Stone could hear a lot of noise in the background, including the telltale snap-pop-crackle of flames. Men shouted, sirens blared, and it just generally sounded like chaos on the other end of the line. Fox had to half-yell into the phone to make himself heard.

"Thought you'd want to know," Fox continued, "that we're out here at the Gunther place." A slight hesitation, then, "It's pretty bad, sheriff."

Stone's gut tightened and his blood ran cold. The Gunthers were long-time members of the Faith Bible Church congregation, their family having attended the church going back five generations. "How bad?" he asked.

"We have Vince here. He's safe."

"What about Cynthia, his wife?"

Fox drew in a deep breath and exhaled slowly before he replied, "Sorry, sheriff, but she didn't make it."

Stone felt an invisible, iron-hard fist punch him deep down where the hurting happens. He tried to ignore the pain as he said, "I'll be right there."

TWO

STONE JUMPED into the Blazer and drove out to the Gunthers as fast as he could, headlights cutting through the evening darkness while the emergency lights flashed in red-blue pulses to clear the road ahead.

Stone had wandered into Whisper Falls a year ago to audition for the head pastor position at Faith Bible Church. After the tragic loss of his seven-year-old daughter—who died after being thrown from a snake-bit horse—and subsequent divorce, he had retired from his "warrior days" as a government black ops specialist.

Hungry for peace after years on the killing fields, he had hoped to become a man of God instead of a man of war.

But when he arrived in town, he discovered Whisper Falls had a dark, evil underbelly. He had put down his Bible, strapped on his guns, and destroyed that evil in a firestorm of blood and thunder. His return to violence culminated in him secretly executing the kid-raping, child-killing former sheriff, vigilante style.

When the gun-smoke cleared, he found himself

wearing the badge, a man of God at times, a warrior at others, and always willing to resort to primal methods in the name of justice.

He still struggled to find a balance. Maybe he always would. It was just something that he needed to learn to live with.

Yeah, right, he thought. *Easier said than done.*

The Gunthers lived in an old farmhouse on a back-road that cut between Whisper Falls and the next town over. The barn out back looked like a swaybacked nag, roof drooping, the boards weathered and half-rotten. Any red paint that once existed was long gone, replaced by patches of green moss and wood fungus. The fallow fields had gone to brush, weeds and saplings choking the soil. The Gunthers got by on government assistance these days, their farming years now a part of Garrison County history.

The house belched black smoke to the heavens. Flames licked from the windows as Stone pulled in behind a cluster of emergency vehicles. He spotted the fire marshal heading his way, holding a fire axe in one hand and a portable radio in the other.

"Thanks for coming, sheriff," Fox greeted as Stone climbed out of the Blazer. "Though right about now I'm guessing Vince needs your pastor skills more than your cop skills."

"No doubt." Stone spotted Vince Gunther, swaddled in a blue blanket, perched in the doorway of an ambulance as a paramedic tended to him.

"I'd bet my next paycheck this fire was deliberate," Fox said.

"You're thinking arson?"

"No proof. Not yet, anyway. Just a gut feeling. But yeah, that's what I'm thinking." Fox canted the fire axe over his shoulder. "Once the burn's been contained, I can get inside and start poking around. I'll let you know if we find anything."

"Appreciate it." As Fox headed back to the blaze, Stone made his way over to Vince Gunther. His soul felt heavy. No matter how many times he comforted people in their time of grief, it never got any easier.

Vince and Cynthia had been among the first to welcome Stone to Whisper Falls. They had been married for better than fifty years and by all accounts, the marriage had been strong and affectionate. They were a modest, down-to-earth, kind-hearted couple who somehow seemed removed from the tragedies of modern life.

Until now.

"Hey, Vince." Stone leaned against the ambulance door. "How you holding up?"

Vince Gunther raised his soot-streaked face. His expression—or rather, lack thereof—caught Stone by surprise. No tears, no anguish, no stress showed on his weathered, craggy features. Just a dull blankness, eyes turned inward as if Vince was trying to stare at something buried deep down in his soul.

"Think I'm just in shock right now, preacher." Gunther spoke so quietly that Stone had to lean closer to catch the words. "Not exactly sure what to say. Cynthia was taking a nap in the sunroom and all of a sudden..." His voice trailed off as he shrugged beneath the blanket.

"What happened?" Stone prompted.

"Don't rightly know." Gunther shook his head slowly. "I've been on blood pressure medication and I'm still getting used to it. Sometimes when I take the pills, the world starts spinning a bit, especially on an empty stomach, so I try to be careful. Took one right before dinner, figuring if I got a little dizzy it wouldn't matter much 'cause I'd be eating soon."

"What then?"

"Started feeling all lightheaded and woozy. Sat down, laid my head on the kitchen table, and next thing I knew, the house was on fire."

"Any idea where it started?" Stone asked.

Gunther shook his head again. "I don't know."

Stone glanced over to where a body laid on a gurney with a sheet draped over it. Cynthia Gunther had been a small, slight woman so it didn't take much to cover her up. Stone didn't need to go over and have a look. He had seen burnt corpses before and they weren't pleasant. Not that death ever was.

He would let the coroner and funeral director deal with the dead. Right now he needed to focus on the living.

"Vince, we'll find a place for you to stay," Stone said. "And I'll take care of the funeral arrangements. You just try to make peace with it, if you can. Call if you need anything."

Gunther didn't seem to hear him and said nothing in reply. Just stared into nowhere, into some internal abyss, his eyes glazed and unfocused, muscles slack and hopeless. Stone stared at him grimly. Vince Gunther might have survived the inferno that took his wife, but the spark of life had vacated his body, leaving behind a broken husk of a man.

Stone stepped back and studied the scene. The firefighters were getting control of the blaze, the former black smoke now thinning to gray streaks that climbed skyward. Keeping well back, Stone walked the perimeter of the wreckage.

He had faced death hundreds of times, had seen men shot, knifed, drowned, blown apart, crushed. But something about fire unsettled him. Not fear—not the sort of thing that gnaws at a man's nerves and weakens him— but something else, something primal, maybe even prehistoric. Something left over from humanity's cave-dwelling days.

His eyes fell on a 2x4 still burning in the blackened ruins of the house. Flames danced with lethal elegance along the wood's charred edge, seeming like an intelligent, living thing.

He had seen men burn and it was one of the worst sorts of death he could imagine, full of pain and horror. He didn't even want to think about how Cynthia Gunther must have felt in her final, agonizing moments as the flames crawled around her and snuffed out her life.

Yeah, Stone acknowledged, sometimes it was hard not to think of fire as a dangerous, mysterious, sentient creature. One that devoured without mercy.

One of the firemen aimed a hose at the engulfed board and extinguished it with a spray of water. Stone stared at the hissing smoke for several long heartbeats, imagining that Hell must look something like this.

Of course, Vince Gunther's hell had only just begun.

With a heavy heart, Stone returned to his Blazer and headed back into town.

———

Needing a pick-me-up, Stone swung over to the Birch Bark Diner. It was well past peak dinner time and the parking lot was nearly empty. Once inside, he took a seat at the counter.

"Howdy, cowboy," Holly Bennet greeted him with an exaggerated, teasing Texas drawl. She grabbed a menu and moseyed over and Stone would have sworn on a stack of Bibles that there was a little extra swing in her hips. "How are you?"

"Been better," Stone answered honestly. He and Holly had fallen into an easy friendship soon after he arrived in town and they had grown closer last winter after he took out the survivalist group that had been terrorizing Holly and her daughter Lizzy. They shared a close bond, but always stopped short of crossing the bridge into something more romantic. They never actually talked about it; it just seemed like some kind of unspoken agreement between them.

"I've got a funeral to plan," he explained. "Cynthia Gunther passed away tonight."

"I'm sorry to hear that." Holly frowned as she poured him a cup of coffee. "She and her husband went to your church, right?"

"Yeah." He took a sip, grateful for the warmth and the kick of caffeine. "Their house burned down. She didn't make it out."

"Really?" Holly's eyebrows arched. "That's the second fire this week."

"Where was the other one?"

"You didn't hear about it?"

"No."

"Old hunting shack out in the woods. Lizzy actually saw it." Holly poured herself a half-cup and leaned across the counter toward him as she sipped. It gave him an intoxicating hint of her perfume, something clean and bright that managed to cut through the cooking smells. "She's friends with Luisa, that girl whose parents came up on the migrant worker program."

"The Valdez family." Stone nodded. "I've met them. They were there at the fire?"

"Not the whole family—just Lizzy and Luisa. They

were out hiking." Holly shrugged. "They said the shack was pretty much done burning when they saw it."

Stone shook his head. "Fire...sometimes it almost seems alive, you know?"

"Guess I never thought about it." Holly looked at him with concern in her eyes. "You all right?"

"I'm fine. Just processing Cynthia's death, I guess."

"I feel so bad for poor Vince, losing his wife like that."

"That's the thing," Stone said. "He didn't seem all that torn up about it."

"Shock does weird things to people."

"I guess. Maybe he'll shake it off, maybe he won't." Stone shrugged. "Time will tell. Anyway, I'm glad to hear Lizzy made a new friend."

"She's not the only one." Holly's eyes twinkled with the devilish mischief of hot gossip. "Have you met Yvonne Brossard yet?"

"Can't say that I have."

"Trust me, you'll know her when you see her. Hot, blonde, gorgeous, and very, very French."

"She's new in town?"

"She's Mason Xavier's new girlfriend."

"That right?" Stone mulled over this news, thinking that it really didn't affect him much, if at all. Mason Xavier was Whisper Falls' richest man, a real pillar of the community, despite countless, unshakeable rumors that significant portions of his wealth originated from illicit activities. "Is she French-from-France, or French-from-Canada?"

"French-Canadian. From Quebec. She runs a company that produces a line of expensive kitchenware. Very high-end. Bloo, it's called."

"Blue?"

"Bloo." She accentuated the vowels, drawing them out. "Two o's."

"How chic," Stone drawled dryly. He drained his coffee and then asked, "You bought any?"

Holly laughed. "On a waitress' salary? Not hardly. A single plate costs, like, a hundred bucks."

"For that kind of money, I'll stick with paper plates."

"Smart man." Holly smiled.

But not smart enough to take the next step and make you mine, Stone thought.

THREE

THAT MASON XAVIER'S new girlfriend hailed from Canada wasn't that much of a surprise. Situated in northern New York, the town of Whisper Falls was a mere 50 miles from the Canadian border and Ontario and Quebec license plates were a common sight in Garrison County.

Being so close to the border, Stone occasionally encountered Canadian lawbreakers jumping over the international boundary and vice-versa. When that happened, he worked in cooperation with the Royal Canadian Mounted Police to deal with the problem.

So it wasn't out of the ordinary when he received a call from his northern neighbors the next morning. He was reviewing the file on Scooby's arrest when Valentine poked his head through the office door.

"Hey, sheriff," the red-haired deputy said. "You've got a call from Captain Chandler."

"Thanks. Put him through." Stone closed the file and got ready to take the call. Captain Chandler worked for the National Security Enforcement Service of the RCMP, the branch that dealt with any police business outside of Canada, including cross-border issues.

The forwarded call came through and Stone picked up the phone. "This is Stone."

"Sheriff Stone." Chandler had a pleasant voice but Stone knew he could be a rough son of a bitch when the situation called for it. "Thanks for taking my call. How are things down there in Garrison County?"

"Not bad. Just small-town stuff. Starting to see an upswing in narcotics, though. You?"

"Yeah, we're seeing it, too." Chandler sighed, the sound tinged with frustration. "I miss the old days when it was just the cartels. Nowadays we're seeing a lot more domestic manufacturing, if you know what I mean."

"I hear that," Stone said. "Picked up a shoplifter last night who had enough cold medicine on him to sink a battleship."

"Ever since *Breaking Bad*, everyone wants to be a meth cook."

"Let's hear it for junk television." Stone laughed. "What can I do for you, captain?"

"Following up on a missing vehicle report," said Chandler. "We got word that a car we're looking for was found in your neck of the woods."

"What kind of car?"

"2019 Honda Civic. Blue. New York license plates. Kilo-Juliet-Lima-five-seven-one."

"Yeah, we've got it," Stone said. "Just got the call a couple hours ago. Guess you Mounties don't let the grass grow under your hooves."

"We've been keeping our eyes and ears open." Chandler's tone was serious. "That car was involved in a homicide in Toronto last week."

"I've got a deputy on scene as we speak," Stone said. "Last I knew, they were waiting for a tow truck."

"I can be there with a truck in two hours."

"Sounds good. I'll make sure the paperwork's in order."

"Thanks, sheriff."

"No problem. See you soon."

———

Ninety minutes later, Stone drove the Blazer deep into the woods, following the old gravel road that wound its way through the trees. This northwestern sector of Garrison County was heavily forested with a mix of beech, pine, and the occasional oak or maple. Despite the cold, he rolled down his window to savor the woody scents and drink in the fresh air.

This particular road actually continued out of Stone's jurisdiction and into Clinton County before dead-ending just shy of the Canadian border. Forest Rangers patrolled the area, which was popular for legitimate pastimes like hiking and hunting as well as not-so-legitimate activities like poaching and smuggling.

Stone thought that when they coined the expression "out in the sticks," this might be the place they had in mind. He hadn't seen any sign of humanity for the last twelve miles.

He navigated the Blazer around a wide curve and when the road straightened again, he saw the Civic up ahead, pulled off to the side beneath the shelter of some pine boughs. Stone pulled in behind and shut off the engine. The metal almost immediately began to tick as it began the cool down process, no doubt aided by the cold autumn air.

The Civic looked to be in relatively good shape. Paint job, tires, and chassis all looked fine and Stone couldn't see any apparent damage as he circled the vehicle. No indication why it was parked out here in the middle of nowhere. A scattering of dead pine needles littered the roof and hood.

Affixed to the windshield was a towing notice. Stone put in a quick call to the ranger whose name was on the ticket to let them know the car was being removed by law enforcement.

Captain Chandler showed up twenty minutes later, driving an RCMP Crown Victoria and leading a flatbed tow truck. They were accompanied by a State Police escort.

Chandler pulled in behind the Blazer and climbed out of his cruiser, pausing to stretch before heading over to Stone. He was a tall man, slender and balding, who looked more like a college professor than a cop. He wore a blue RCMP bomber jacket and the distinctive navy-blue pants with yellow stripe.

"Thanks for your help on this, sheriff." Chandler shook Stone's hand. "We've been looking for this car."

"You said it was part of a homicide investigation." Stone leaned against the Blazer as the tow truck operator got to work hooking up the Civic. A red squirrel in a nearby tree chattered its irritation at them.

Chandler nodded. "Nasty business. Shootout at a night club in Toronto on a Saturday night, about two weeks back. A couple of rival gangs decided to go to war right there on the dancefloor. Being the weekend, it was packed. Four dead, nine wounded. Place looked like a damned slaughterhouse."

"You figure out what made them go to guns?"

"Turf war over drugs." Chandler shook his head. "Crystal meth, to be precise. It's been a major problem in the cities for a while and now the rural areas have started to get in on the action."

"Must make you Mounties long for the good ol'

days," Stone said. "Out on the prairie, chasing down whiskey traders, campfire nights under the stars."

"More like mosquitos, dysentery, and malnutrition," Chandler replied. "Nah, I'll stick with my comfy air-conditioned office and dual-monitor computer, thanks. How the hell Mounties ever functioned before Starbucks is beyond me."

The tow truck operator hoisted the Civic onto the rear platform and secured it. Stone and Chandler watched as the guy ratcheted down the heavy duty straps to hold the car firmly in place.

"Looks like we can take it from here," Chandler said.

"No doubt. How'd you find out we had the car, anyway?"

"Civilian reported it to the forest rangers. Rangers relayed it to the State Police. State Police notified us. This close to the border, the RCMP and New York State Police have a pretty good working relationship."

"Makes sense."

"It was reported by some guy named..." Chandler pulled out a small notebook and checked his scribblings. "Dale. Dale Michaels. Told the rangers he lives around here."

"He does." Stone felt suspicion rise within him. "He's a local meth-head. Not the one we arrested yesterday but he runs with the same crowd."

Chandler's eyebrows shot up. "Junkies don't usually tip off the cops unless there's something in it for them."

"I know," Stone said. "That's what worries me."

FOUR

STONE WORKED at the sheriff's station until noon, wolfed down a sandwich, then headed over to the church. He had a funeral to plan.

Faith Bible Church was a modest building, complete with the traditional steeple and painted the traditional white, located outside of town. It sort of looked like the kind of church you would have found in a boomtown during the gold rush days, though it had actually been built in the 1960s.

Stone tossed his coat and Stetson in the office and then headed to the small kitchenette to make a pot of coffee. He had a half-hour until David White, his head deacon, arrived with Vince Gunther. The widow Unser had also agreed to come and hopefully serve as a steadying influence on the bereaved.

Dealing with death always made Stone think about the loss of his daughter. There were plenty of Bible verses out there to help grieving people through troubled times, but one of his favorites was Romans 8:35.

Who will separate us from the love of Christ? Will hardship,
or distress, or persecution, or famine, or nakedness, or peril, or
sword?

The heart of any man whose wife had just been taken from him was bound to be hardening, or would be soon. In some ways, it was just a natural part of the grieving process, an emotional defense mechanism. God knew Stone's heart had hardened after he buried Jasmine. No matter how hard you tried not to let it, grief changed a man. Even wounds that heal leave a scar behind. Sometimes faith was the only thing that carried you through the storm.

…neither death, nor life, nor angels, nor rulers, nor things
present, nor things to come, nor powers, nor height, nor depth,
nor anything else in all creation, will be able to separate us
from the love of God.

Faith could make all the difference in the world, Stone knew. Faith could give a bereaved man the strength to carry on when all he wanted to do was crawl into a hole and die.

"Stone? You here?"

Stone recognized David White's voice. Despite being the head deacon, White flat-out refused to call him "pastor." Not that Stone cared, but he recognized the omission for the intended slight that it was. White disapproved of Stone's unorthodox methods of pastoring and found bitter satisfaction in being the proverbial thorn in the side.

With a longsuffering sigh, Stone headed for the chapel. He found White there, trying to have a heart-to-heart with Vince Gunther as the widower stared blankly at the large wooden cross hanging on the wall behind the pulpit.

"We're all here for you, Vince," White was saying. "No matter the time, whatever the need, don't hesitate to call."

Gunther shook his head like he was trying to rouse himself from a daydream. He glanced at White and grunted an acknowledgement, but said nothing more.

Stone stepped forward and put a hand on Gunther's shoulder. "How you doing today, Vince?"

Deacon White jumped in before Gunther even had a chance to respond. "We're all very concerned for Mr. Gunther's well-being. Those of us who've been here for *years* feel the loss of Cynthia deeply, in a way that a newcomer could never understand. It's the kind of thing that comes from knowing someone a long time, of being connected with them and the community."

Stone didn't take the bait. White had fancied himself the heir apparent to the pastor position and was angered to find his plans derailed when Stone rode into town. Stone's popularity among the parishioners only added salt to the wound. As petty retaliation, White rarely passed up a chance to emphasize Stone's new-guy-in-town status.

"I don't think you needed to know Cynthia long to be touched by her," Stone replied. "Vince, can I get you a cup of coffee?"

"No, thanks." Gunther was eerily calm, almost as if he was indifferent to everything.

The widow Unser arrived with a pan of homemade coffee cake and immediately took a motherly interest in Gunther, putting an arm around him protectively.

"Vince, we're here for you," she said quietly. "When my husband died all those years ago, I wouldn't have got through it without this church."

"We remember." White nodded.

"David White, don't be ridiculous." Widow Unser snorted derisively. "You weren't even living here yet and quite frankly, more often than not, we wish you *still* weren't living here."

Stone intervened before White's wounded look could escalate into angry words. Despite her sweet, grandma-like nature, widow Unser often deployed a sharp tongue, with little patience for foolishness, and White had a tendency to slash back when his pride took a blow. "Why don't we go sit down in my office?" Stone suggested.

They reconvened in Stone's office. The widow Unser stopped by the kitchenette to get some plates and cutlery for the cake. As she cut a piece and handed it to Gunther, she asked, "Did Cynthia have anything special in mind for her service?"

He sighed and shook his head. "No. I mean, not really, not that I know of. We never really talked about it."

Stone found that strange. In his experience, most people the Gunthers' age had expressed to their spouses or family some indication of what they wanted at their funeral. Then again, not all wives and husbands were comfortable conversing about death. Some people seemed to think that if you never talked about it, then it would never happen. They were wrong, of course. The Reaper comes for everyone in the end.

"How about Bible verses?" Stone asked. "She have any favorites?"

"Well, let me think on that for a second." Vince stared out the window, reminding Stone of a student longing for the end of a school day. After a too-long silence, he said, "She really liked the one about the lilies in the field … or at least, I think she did." A disinterested shrug. "Not sure."

"Okay." Stone jotted down the verse. "How about music? What songs did she like?"

The pause that followed was even longer than the first, dragging on into uncomfortable awkwardness as Gunther appeared to be struggling with his memory. But as the silence deepened, he seemed to just give up and resumed staring blankly out the window.

White cleared his throat. "Did she like hymns, Vince? Contemporary Christian? Country music?"

Gunther slowly turned his head and seemed to look at each of them as if trying to remember who they were and why he was here. "Don't much care about the music," he finally said. He abruptly rose to his feet. "I need some fresh air, if you don't mind."

"Sure," Stone said. "Dave, will you take Vince outside?"

"Of course." White stood up and headed for the door. "This way, Vince."

Once the two men had left the room, the widow Unser turned to Stone and said, "Poor man. He seems really out of it."

"Grief can do that to a person."

"Pastor, were you aware…" Her voice trailed off and she looked down at her lap, fidgeting with her hands. "Maybe I should just keep quiet."

"Little late for that," Stone said, not unkindly. "Aware of what?"

"Vince and Cynthia." She sighed. "They were having some problems."

"Really? They've been married forever."

"Old people can have marriage problems, too," the widow Unser replied. "Sometimes it's even worse than young folks' because of a good, long simmering. Then one day the stew pot finally boils over and look out."

"Yeah, that makes sense."

"From what I've gathered, for the last year or so, the two of them just stopped talking to each other." She shook her head. "So very sad."

Stone agreed. Before his daughter's death, he had enjoyed a happy marriage with Theresa, so he knew open communication was vital to a healthy relationship.

He was about to say something along those lines when his cell phone vibrated. He checked the screen and saw that it was the station calling. "Sorry," he said to the widow Unser. "I have to take this."

She nodded her understanding. "You carry two crosses, pastor. Not sure how you do it, but God bless you."

Stone answered the phone. "This is Stone."

"Sheriff, we just got a call from Dennis Fox." Deputy Valentine spoke fast, the words coming out in a rush. "There's been another fire."

FIVE

STONE GOT directions from Valentine and headed out into the forest north of Whisper Falls. The woods were a tourist's paradise for three seasons, before the snow hit and closed the trails to everyone but the cross-country skiers and snow-shoe enthusiasts. This late in the fall, the autumn foliage had dropped from the trees and covered the ground in a carpet of brittle brown leaves.

Stone followed a dirt logging road around the back of a hardwood ridge. The afternoon sunlight tried to stream through the barren branches but got blocked by the foul black smoke billowing into the sky. As he neared the scene, he saw the cluster of firetrucks and emergency vehicles parked on the shoulder.

An RV, set back in a clearing, smouldered fitfully. The fire crew flooded its blackened, skeletal frame with water. Luckily the RV had been far enough away from the trees to avoid starting a forest fire.

Dennis Fox came over, soot streaking his face like war paint. "We have to stop meeting like this, sheriff."

"What can I say, Fox? You get me all fired up."

Fox groaned. "That was a terrible joke."

"That's the kind I'm best at," Stone replied with a grin. "What've we got here?"

"Nothing good, believe me. Once it cools down, you can come take a look."

Stone sat around for over an hour as the firefighters doused the RV with enough water to float Noah's Ark. No chance of even a single spark surviving the deluge and the cold water eventually cooled the scorched metal.

A fireman started to cordon off the area with yellow tape as Fox waved Stone over. Stone walked across the hose-strewn ground, dead grass stomped flat by an endless parade of boots, the earth churned to mud.

"No more hot spots," Fox said as Stone approached. "Should be safe enough to let you in for the three dollar tour."

Stone glanced at the burned-out remains of the RV. It was a total loss. "Any bodies?"

"No, thank God." Fox scrunched up his face in a look of disgust. "Bodies smell like shit when they cook." He paused, then added, "Well, maybe not like shit, exactly, but it's definitely unpleasant."

Stone knew exactly what he meant. The scent of a charred corpse was a unique stench, one not easily forgotten. He always associated it with a mission in Egypt, where some Coptic Christians had been burned alive by members of the Daesh-Sinai terrorist group. Stone had been too late to save them—a failure that still haunted him—but not too late to avenge their deaths. As far as he knew, the bones of the terrorists were still buried in the western desert sands.

He followed Fox into the burnt husk of the trailer, entering through what had been the front room. The place was an absolute wreck. The couch had sizzled down to blackened springs.

Stone stepped past and went into the kitchen area

where the stove, sink, and countertop were crowded with equipment. Fox pointed at a container with a small glass protrusion. Stone recognized it as a pressure cooker.

Next Fox opened a metal cabinet and pointed inside. Stone saw a blue plastic container, partially melted, adorned with a badly-burned and barely-recognizable biohazard symbol.

Stone was starting to put it all together and what it added up to was nothing good. Pressure cookers and volatile chemicals were the kind of combination that made things go boom.

The back bedroom area looked like it had been converted into some sort of workplace. Smoke, burn, and water damage had reduced it to a blackened wreckage. In the middle of the mess, Stone saw the melted remains of scales and a shrink-wrap press.

"Don't touch the counter," Fox warned. "Unless you want to go back to your office with a nasty chemical burn."

"Thanks for the heads-up."

The two men went back outside where Fox said, "I'm sure I don't have to tell you this, but I think we're looking at a meth lab that blew up."

"Looks like it," Stone agreed. "But I would have expected a body."

Fox shrugged. "If you wanted me to hazard a guess, I'd say the cook got lucky and stepped outside for a smoke or a piss or something when the shit exploded. Sometimes God favors fools."

"The rain falls on the just and the unjust," Stone said. He gestured at the burned-out remains of the RV. "Do we know who owned that thing yet?"

"No license plate and if there was a registration in the glovebox, it went up in smoke. But I can tell that this particular parcel of land is privately owned."

"That's a lucky break." Stone knew it was unusual to find private property this far back in the wilderness. Most of the deep woods were state-controlled as part of the Forest Reserve and regulated by the Adirondack Park Agency. "So who owns it?"

Fox fished out a notepad. "A Canadian. Yvonne Brossard."

Shit, Stone thought. Mason Xavier's new girlfriend.

SIX

MASON XAVIER WAS ABOUT AS slippery as a catfish slathered in Vaseline.

Seemed like every town had someone like him. Back in the old days, they called dirty power players like that a "wheel." What the current term was, Stone had no idea. He just thought of them as scumbags. Not exactly a charitable or Christ-like opinion, but when it came to such things, Stone knew he was more sinner than saint.

As Stone drove the Blazer back to town, he pondered how money always seemed to lend a veneer of legitimacy to whatever it touched, no matter how filthy. All too often, wealth cloaked evil deeds.

Mason Xavier always seemed to be skirting the edges of whatever illicit activity was going on in Garrison County. The latest rumor claimed he was involved with the importation of illegal labor into the country. And Stone still suspected Xavier had financed the survivalists who had kidnapped, raped, and murdered young girls in the area last year. The former sheriff, Grant Camden, had been involved in that nasty business as well. Stone had exterminated the survivalists and fed the sheriff to the coy-wolves that roamed the area, but Xavier had skated clear without so much a smudge.

Stone was perfectly willing to kill in the name of justice, but not without hard proof. Suspicions of Xavier's fingers being dipped in criminal activity weren't enough to drop the hammer on him.

Still, Stone didn't like the guy, not one bit. Time to pay him a visit.

———

Mason Xavier lived on a mansion estate atop a large hill that overlooked Whisper Falls, a pseudo-king looking down on his would-be kingdom. There was no denying that the man wielded considerable power and influence in this town. Stone had been warned to tread lightly in his dealings with Xavier...and some of those warnings had come directly from Xavier himself.

Too bad treading lightly wasn't really Stone's style.

He pulled up to the gate at the bottom of the hill. Large granite pillars framed the driveway, between which stretched a ten-foot high black iron gate on rollers. Recessed into one of the pillars was an intercom panel. Stone pressed the button and waited.

At least two full minutes went by before a man's voice, sounding snooty to Stone's ears, finally answered: "May I help you?"

"Sheriff Stone to see Mr. Xavier."

A long pause, then: "I see. Do you have an appointment?"

"Maybe you missed the part where I mentioned I'm the sheriff," Stone replied. "Where's Xavier?"

"I'm Carlton." Now the man sounded both snooty and annoyed. "Mr. Xavier's personal assistant. Is there something I can do for you?"

"Yeah, you can tell me where Xavier is."

The pause that followed was probably even longer than two minutes. Stone could practically feel the irritation coming through the intercom speaker. He didn't give a damn. He sat in the Blazer and waited Carlton out. Worst case scenario, he would just ram the gate open with his truck.

He shifted into gear and got ready to do just that when he heard an electronic click and the gate rumbled open.

"You may proceed up to the house." Carlton's sneering tone made it clear that he felt a peasant was being granted an audience with the king.

Stone rolled through the gate and steered the Blazer up the long hill. The driveway was made of reinforced concrete imprinted with a clamshell pattern. Neatly-trimmed evergreen hedges spaced between decorative boulders lined the sides.

The drive ascended straight up the hill—it had to be a real bear coming down that slope in icy weather—before curving around to a large plateau at the top. To the side of the house was a helicopter pad but Stone didn't see any helicopter. Maybe it was in the shop for repairs.

The house itself looked like something from a Hollywood film. Not a James Bond-esque villain's lair exactly; more of a hacienda vibe, something that looked like it would be more at home in Tucson than a small mountain town in upstate New York. It was easily the most lavish estate in Whisper Falls, rivaling even some of the multi-million dollar spreads over in Lake Placid.

Stone climbed out of the Blazer and walked over to the thick wooden doors set underneath a stone archway. No need to knock; they opened as soon as he approached.

"Sheriff Stone." The man who stood in the doorway was slight, balding, and clad in an impeccably-tailored, beige-colored, three-piece suit. "I'm Carlton. May I ask what this intrusion—I mean, this *visit*—is in regards to?"

"Sure, you can ask. But you won't get an answer."

Carlton frowned his disapproval. "You're being difficult, sheriff."

"It's only going to get worse until your boss shows up."

"Of course. Mr. Xavier should be out momentarily. In the meantime, I have been instructed to offer you refreshment. Would you care for a drink?"

Stone could still taste soot in his mouth from the burnt RV and thought a cold glass of Jack and Coke, lots of ice, easy on the Jack, would do a fine job of washing it away. But not while he was on duty. "No," he said. "I'm good."

"Then right this way, sheriff."

Stone followed Carlton through a glass doorway into a vast split-level common area dominated by a fireplace so large, you could have spit-roasted a bison in it. In the center of the room rested a glass coffee table surrounded by a couch and chairs.

As Carlton wandered off to fetch his master, Stone examined the books on the table. One was a photographic collection of Frank Lloyd Wright buildings. Another chronicled *The Wonders of British Columbia*. The third was simply labeled Bloo and he plucked it from the pile.

It was a thick book, expensively bound, full of photographs, and must have cost a fortune to produce. Sumptuously designed in patterns of soft white and eggshell blue, the thick pages sported artsy pictures of luxury kitchenware.

The Bloo collection featured a distinctive logo—two curved lines intersecting to suggest a minimalist half-shell shape supporting a stylized "B." The product line encompassed plates, glassware, and cutlery, not to mention equipment like toasters, kettles, and crockpots. Everything was characterized by a hexagonal motif.

Stone wasn't much for fancy things but he recognized quality when he saw it. The book contained no prices, a sure sign that the merchandise was expensive. No point in giving the casual viewer a dose of sticker shock.

He flipped the Bloo book over and looked at the photo of a gorgeous woman on the back cover. Blonde hair styled in a page-boy cut and dressed in a retro-styled power suit with padded shoulders, the lady possessed the facial features of the classic French minx. Eyes narrowed and lips seductively twisted into a knowing smirk, she stared out of the picture with arms crossed, her posture something of a come-hither dare or challenge. Stone's eyes dropped from her sultry features to read the accompanying text below.

YVONNE BROSSARD is the founder and CEO of Bloo™, which was founded in 2016. She and her company have won multiple business and humanitarian awards. She is featured in the book *Trailblazers: Canadian Women Entrepreneurs*. She holds an MBA from Yale with a specialty in marketing and communications.

"Sheriff Stone. What a pleasant surprise."

Stone closed the book and set it back down on the table. Mason Xavier approached, glossy smile affixed to his Hollywood-handsome face, hair perfectly gelled. He wore a pollen-yellow robe and sandals, a towel slung over one shoulder.

"Bit cold for a day at the beach," Stone said.

"I have an indoor heated pool," Xavier replied.

Of course you do, Stone thought. "Well, thanks for taking the time to talk to me."

"Based on what Carlton relayed to me, I got the impression that I did not have much of a choice. But of course, I'm always happy to help our local law enforcement." Xavier's tone was as fake as his smile. "Now, please, tell me what this is all about."

Stone settled his honey-colored eyes on the man. "I understand Yvonne Brossard is staying with you."

"That's correct. Is there a problem?"

"There was a fire on the property she owns north of town. I need to talk to her about it."

"A fire? My God, that's terrible news. Was anybody hurt?"

"Doesn't look like it."

"Well, I guess that's the silver lining in the cloud. If you wait here, I'll go fetch Yvonne. Be right back."

Stone appreciated Xavier's willingness to cooperate. That hadn't always been the case. In the wake of the scandal involving the survivalists and their child-hunting activities, Xavier had stonewalled with high-priced lawyers, providing the minimal amount of information necessary to avoid suspicion. Despite all the rumors and his reputation for being involved in unsavory dealings, Xavier was like a mink, always able to keep his coat spotless.

A few minutes later, Yvonne Brossard made her grand entrance.

She cut a commanding figure as she stalked into the room, not a hair out of place, a haughty smirk on her beautiful face that peeked out from her blonde tresses. It was the kind of face that didn't need much makeup to look stunning.

She wore a white dress shirt with the sleeves rolled up and the top three buttons undone to show a generous but not salacious amount of cleavage. Her black silk slacks were loose and billowy around her legs. She held a hard-cover book in one hand, a finger inserted as a place-marker so she wouldn't lose her page. As if she expected to be done with Stone in less than two minutes and get back to her reading.

She moved with balance and a subtle eroticism, striking a pose with a hip thrown forward and her free hand on her tiny waist. Part she-wolf, part temptress, and every inch a danger from the crown of her head to the soles of her bare feet.

"So you're the sheriff." She chuckled, low and throaty. "You even have a cowboy hat and everything. How charming."

Stone glanced at the book in her hand. *The Art of War* by Sun-Tzu. "That's some heavy reading you've got there."

She smiled, though it never reached her eyes. "I'm guessing you're more of a *Guns & Ammo* kind of guy."

"The Bible is more like it," Xavier said. "The sheriff also happens to be a preacher."

Yvonne arched her immaculately-manicured eyebrows as her steely gaze measured up Stone. "So you're more of a God-and-guns kind of guy."

"Guilty as charged."

"Well, sheriff, what's so important that it made you come all the way up here?"

"You own some property in the northern part of the county?"

"Yes."

"The trailer you had there burned down and the fire looks suspicious. There was evidence of criminal activity."

"Trailer?" Yvonne frowned. "I don't know anything about a trailer."

"Seriously?"

Yvonne Brossard's gaze hardened dangerously. This was not a woman to be teased or trifled with, Stone warned himself. She fancied herself an important person with little time for people she considered beneath her. She was a huntress exuding barracuda vibes.

"Yes, Sheriff Stone, I am serious." Her tone was clipped, exasperated. "I don't know anything about trailers on my land, so there's no way I could know about suspicious fires or criminal activity." Her eyes flashed at him. "Are you accusing me of something?"

"No," Stone said, silently adding, *Not yet.* "But the fact remains there was a thirty-foot RV parked on your property."

"Like I've already said, I have no idea how it got there. It isn't mine."

"When was the last time you were out there?"

"Last week." Yvonne studiously avoided looking at Xavier when she said it.

Stone glanced over at Garrison County's wealthiest citizen and saw a disapproving frown crease his face. Looked like he hadn't known about any of this, and Mason Xavier was a man who liked to be in control. Surprises were not something he enjoyed. Stone wondered what else Yvonne hadn't told him, and Xavier was probably wondering the same thing.

Carlton's voice floated down the hall, getting closer. "…in here with Mr. Xavier and Ms. Brossard." He entered the room. "Pardon the interruption, everyone. Sheriff, your deputy is here." He stepped aside and Valentine brushed past him.

"Sheriff. Mr. Xavier." The deputy nodded in greeting, a polite smile on his face. The smile brightened considerably when he laid eyes on Yvonne. "Ma'am," he said, sweeping his hat off his head and gracing her with a nod so big it practically turned into a bow.

Yvonne Brossard watched this display of awkward, boyish gallantry with amusement. "A cop with manners," she cooed. "You truly are a credit to your profession, deputy."

Stone lowered his head so that the brim of his Stetson hid the smirk on his face. Beyond Yvonne's carefully-cultivated air of cool detachment, he sensed a genuine glimmer of attraction toward his significantly younger deputy. With Valentine's shock of red hair and easygoing charm, it was no surprise that a cougar like Yvonne would be drawn to him.

"Thank you, ma'am," Valentine replied. He blushed just a bit, a fact not lost on Yvonne, who let out a sigh that trilled off at the end to finish as a purr.

Mason Xavier's eyes flicked back and forth between Yvonne and Valentine. "Sheriff," he said, "how many more officers do you plan on bringing? Should I arrange to have extra chairs put out?" The sarcasm was thick. "Maybe have some supper catered?"

"No offense, but I wouldn't eat with you."

"Some people might consider that rude. Out of curiosity, why not?"

"Guilt by association."

Xavier's eyes narrowed slightly. "Since you're a preacher, maybe I should remind you that Jesus ate with sinners. In fact, I think that was kind of a big thing in the Bible."

"Yeah, well, I'm not Jesus."

Xavier smiled coldly. "At least we can agree on that."

Stone looked over at Valentine, who was still gawking at Yvonne like a schoolboy seeing his first nudie magazine. "You got something to tell me?"

"Yes, sir." The deputy shook his head to clear away the spell he'd been under ever since he walked into the room and locked eyes with Yvonne Brossard. "Fire marshal stopped by the station and said it looks like the trailer blaze was arson, not a chemical explosion."

"Chemicals?" Yvonne echoed. "Just what the hell was going on out there?"

"They think someone was maybe using the trailer to cook up some meth," Valentine said.

"My God." Yvonne looked stricken. Whether it was real or fake, Stone couldn't tell, and he had been trained to detect falsehoods. If she was faking, she was damn good at it. "You mean to tell me that someone parked a trailer on my property, cooked up some drugs, and then deliberately set the place on fire?"

"Or someone else set it on fire," Stone said. "We're not sure yet. The investigation is just getting started. Getting a statement from the landowner is the first step."

"She's given you a statement," Xavier said flatly. "We —you—are done here. No more questions."

"Shush, Mason." Yvonne waved a hand at her boyfriend and smiled sweetly at Valentine. "I'll be happy to provide this fine deputy with anything he needs." The smile turned wicked. "Anything at all."

Xavier didn't look happy. "If you feel the need to give a statement, then give it to Sheriff Stone."

"Sorry," Stone said, "but I have to get back to the office." He smiled thinly at Xavier. "Deputy Valentine will be happy to take Ms. Brossard's statement." He touched the brim of his Stetson. "Enjoy the rest of your day. I'll find my own way out."

As Stone moved past him, Xavier hissed under his breath, "You're a fucking asshole."

"Sometimes," Stone agreed, and walked away.

SEVEN

EARLY THE NEXT MORNING, Stone did some checking and learned that Yvonne Brossard was in the United States as a tourist, meaning she could stay in the country for six months without a visa. She had rented a house in town and Stone did a drive-by to check it out.

It was a small cottage on a quiet backstreet with a modest front yard that featured a Crimson King maple tree. The picket fence out front looked freshly painted. It didn't seem like the kind of place that would interest Yvonne Brossard at all, and Stone doubted she spent much time there. Why would she, when she could just zip up to Xavier's mansion for a dip in the heated pool and some hot loving in a king-size bed?

Stone wondered if Yvonne's fascination with Cade Valentine was just a ruse to make Xavier jealous or if she truly was a cougar with a taste for younger men. Maybe big-shot Mason Xavier wasn't doing enough to tend to his lady's intense, insatiable hungers.

Stone chuckled to himself. Maybe one night he would drive by this place and see Valentine's truck parked in the driveway. Hell, maybe it would still be there in the morning. Rumor had it that Valentine made a fantastic egg-white omelette.

Stone was getting ready to pull away from the curb and head to the station when the front door of the cottage opened and someone stepped out.

Scooby.

He grabbed a rake and a plastic garbage bin off the porch. He slouched over to the bare-branched maple tree and started raking the dead leaves into a pile.

Stone's eyes narrowed. The meth-head had just bailed out yesterday and now here he was doing yard work at Yvonne Brossard's place at 7:30 in the morning. Yeah, nothing suspicious about that at all.

Stone decided it was time to call his friend up north and get more information about the smoking-hot she-cat that had just rolled into town.

———

"Yvonne Brossard, hey?" The phone connection to Ontario was remarkably clear, almost like Captain Chandler was sitting right there in Stone's office. "Yeah, she's an interesting character. She on your radar?"

"She owns some land in my neck of the woods," Stone replied. "Trailer on it burned down and it looks like somebody was using it to cook meth."

"Let me guess—no hard evidence that connects her to the cooking."

"Nothing I can slap cuffs on her for."

"Yeah, you're gonna want to tread carefully with that one."

"Why's that?"

"She's very well connected." Stone heard Chandler clicking a mouse as he talked. "Says here she has close associations with heavy industry in Quebec, mainly construction, and has won some business awards. But what will be more interesting to you is that she has mob connections."

"She in deep?"

"Not exactly. She was identified last year in a government wiretap while meeting with a couple of mobsters that were under surveillance by the Canadian Border Service. Turns out she was a minor player. She hired some damn good lawyers and skated clear of any charges."

"What was she mixed up in?"

"Looks like some local-level fraud, mostly. Some money laundering through restaurants...nothing new in Montreal. Prostitution."

"Woman that looks like that is no street-walker," Stone said. "Must have been an escort."

"Looks like she was suspected of working on the procurement side of things. You know, a madam. But nothing concrete and she managed to keep her hands clean."

"So what's your take?" Stone asked.

"From what I can tell, she seems to be a legitimate businesswoman who rubbed up against some less than savory individuals."

"She still mixed up with them?"

"Doesn't seem to be. Looks like she distanced herself once her Bloo business took off. Speaking of Bloo, the company checks out. Everything aboveboard. CSA-compliant, taxes in order, no complaints or violations. She might have a questionable past, but it looks like Yvonne Brossard pulled herself together and went straight."

"She's hooked up with a guy down here named Mason Xavier," Stone said. "Bigshot business-type with a lot of money but rumored to be dirty as hell. Maybe he paid her bail with the mob."

Chandler clacked away on his keyboard. "What was the name again? Mason something?"

"Xavier." Stone spelled it for him.

More typing, then Chandler said, "Did you know he's banned from entering Canada? If he tried to cross at any port of entry, he'd be in trouble."

"Why?"

"Not sure. There are plenty of reasons we won't let someone in the country. But yeah, your boy Mason Xavier is not allowed to enter Canada under any circumstances. If we ever find him on our side of the border, he'll be arrested and sent back to the U.S."

Stone thanked Chandler and hung up, wondering what Xavier had done to wear out his welcome with their northern neighbors.

———

After lunch, Stone switched to preacher mode and decided it was time to meet with the funeral director. Not his favorite thing to do, but it was part of the job. Just like death was part of life.

The Good Fortune Funeral Home—which Stone thought was a stupid, tone-deaf name for a funeral parlor —was located on a side street in town, stuck between a canoe rental shop and an apartment complex. Like all the buildings on this stretch, the place was old but well-kept. The business was run by an eccentric loner named Edgar Julian.

Stone parked on the street in front of the funeral home. Even inside the Blazer, he could feel the air of sorrow that clung to the place like a wet cobweb. The energy here felt dark and miserable, as if everything was coated with ash from the crematory. No surprise, really; nobody came to a funeral home when they were having their best day, and their grieving hearts and broken spirits left an invisible yet indelible mark.

Stone marched up the wide, stone steps. Before he even reached the top, the door creaked open, the hinges crying out for some oil, and Edgar Julian appeared.

"Good afternoon, Pastor Stone, and welcome." Julian was a man of uncertain ancestry, possibly Oriental, possibly African. Tall and slender, he shaved his head and wore impeccably-tailored broadcloth suits. He sported a sharply-trimmed goatee that framed a smiling mouth and steel-rimmed glasses with small, round lenses. He always reminded Stone of Mephistopheles from the Faustian legend. "Please come in."

Julian stepped aside and made a half-bow, sweeping gesture as Stone entered the cavernous entryway. The Good Fortune Funeral Home had operated continuously since the early 1900s and Edgar Julian had been the director for as long as most folks could remember. He was a Whisper Falls fixture; even the widow Unser couldn't remember anyone else ever having run the place.

Julian escorted Stone down a marble hallway to a door disguised as a mirror panel that he opened to reveal a small, dimly-lit office with dark wood on the walls. The room was all shadows and secrets.

"Please, have a seat," Julian said as he wedged himself behind the wooden desk which was too large for the cramped office. He touched a file sitting next to the phone. "The arrangements have all been made for Mrs. Gunther's service. It was her wish to be cremated."

Great, more fire, Stone thought. *It's everywhere. Even among the dead.*

It was hot as hell in the claustrophobic office, the heat cranking from an old cast-iron radiator in the corner. Stone guessed Julian needed it that warm to heat up his old bones, but he found it insufferable. He swept the Stetson off his head and sleeved away the sweat already beading his brow.

"Too warm for you?" Julian asked with a knowing smile.

"Feels like I'm getting tossed in the crematory myself."

"I enjoy it hot." Julian shrugged apologetically but made no move to turn down the heat. "Speaking of which, I hear there's been a number of fires around town recently."

"Small town news travels fast," Stone said.

"That it does, sir." Julian sighed. "Personally, I adore fire, though it must be treated with great care and respect. It has the power to break out and gain control over its master, devouring and digesting and leaving behind nothing but ash. Almost like a living, breathing beast. Tell me, have these fires injured anyone?"

"Other than Cynthia, no."

"Well, let us thank God for that."

Where was God when Cynthia was burning to death? The thought came to Stone unbidden, but he let it ride. He wasn't the kind of preacher who shied away from the tough questions, even when those questions had no easy answers.

Julian continued to speak. "Working with cadavers damaged by fire presents certain challenges where embalming is concerned. Not an issue on this occasion, since Mrs. Gunther opted for cremation."

Stone's cell phone buzzed, alerting him he had received an email. Apologizing to Julian for the intrusion, he took a moment to open the message and saw that it was the coroner's preliminary report. A copy had been sent to Dennis Fox as well. He put the phone back in his pocket. He would read the report later.

Julian rested his elbows on the desk with his hands clasped together in front of him. "A preacher's work is never done, nor is a sheriff's," he said. "I greatly admire your ability to perform both duties. Must be very difficult."

"Some days are better than others," Stone admitted.

"Well." Julian smiled and Stone tried hard not to imagine there was something ghoulish about the grin. "Shall we discuss Mrs. Gunther's final journey?"

"Seems to me her soul already took the trip." Stone shifted in his chair. "What you'll be cremating is her body, nothing more."

"I personally believe the soul and the body are connected," Julian said. "The fire will cleanse the body and free Mrs. Gunther's soul to take her final voyage into whatever life awaits beyond this one. A purging, if you will."

"To be absent from the body is to be present with the Lord." Stone quoted the well-known scripture. "That's what I believe, so I reckon we'll have to agree to disagree."

"We all put our faith in something." Julian nodded his head, either agreeing with Stone's disagreement or simply agreeing with his own statement. "I put my faith in fire and pray it's not the flames of Hell."

"Amen," Stone said, not sure what else to say.

EIGHT

TWO DAYS LATER, Stone was in his church office working on his message for Cynthia Gunther's funeral service, scheduled for that afternoon. The phone rang, interrupting his solemn thoughts. He welcomed the reprieve and snatched up the receiver.

"This is Pastor Stone."

"I don't want *Pastor* Stone, I want *Sheriff* Stone." Mason Xavier sounded like he was all twisted up. "More to the point, I want *Sheriff* Stone to tell me what the hell is going on."

Stone swiveled in his chair to stare out the office window where a few timid snowflakes were drifting down from an ochre-colored sky. "Not sure what you mean."

"Your deputy … what's his name? Valentine? He's been out here two more times to talk to Yvonne."

"Official police business. A known felon was seen at her house. I asked Valentine to follow up."

"Yes, Scooby. A worthless meth-head. Yvonne has a soft heart and takes pity on fools. She hired him to do some yard work at her place. Rake the leaves, mow the lawn, that sort of stuff."

"Right. That's what Valentine told me."

"Do you have to keep sending him?"

"Has he done something wrong?"

"Well, no."

"So what's the problem?"

"I would just prefer that if there are any further questions for Yvonne, you send someone other than Deputy Valentine to ask them. I would consider it a personal favor."

"No promises," said Stone.

"Is that really the best I'm going to get from you?"

Stone let his silence speak for itself.

Xavier sighed heavily, as if the weight of the world was crushing down on his shoulders. "Fine. Honestly, sheriff, I'm not sure why you feel the need to be so difficult. As I've told you before, I make a far better friend than enemy."

"I've got enough friends, and one more enemy won't matter much."

"Fair enough. I'm asking you politely. Just do what you can. Please."

"Like I said, no promises."

"You're a pain in the ass, Stone." Xavier hung up.

Two seconds later, his cell phone rang. The caller ID showed him that it was Captain Chandler from the RCMP. Stone answered immediately.

"Stone here."

"Stone, it's Doug Chandler." He was speaking loud, practically shouting, to be heard over the sound of sirens. "I've got two fugitives on the run, heading your way. Crashed the border by Champlain. We're in pursuit along with Border Patrol and New York State Police, but they're running straight down Route 3, heading right for Whisper Falls."

————

Stone ordered his three on-duty deputies to set up a road block on State Route 3 on the northern edge of the Garrison County line. He informed them it was a high-speed vehicle intercept in support of the RCMP and Homeland Security. They radioed back that they were on it. Then he jumped in the Blazer and tore out of the parking lot, mud and gravel rooster-tailing from the rear tires.

Four vehicles would have to be enough. *Should* be enough, for what he had in mind. He aimed the Blazer north and stomped on the gas, engine surging with all the horsepower it could muster. The deputies knew their jobs and he trusted them to get things ready while he was heading to the scene. He had never been the micro-managing type.

Stone cut loose with the siren, letting its keening wail carve apart the morning air as the Blazer ate up the road. Traffic was light and the few cars he encountered quickly pulled off to the side to let him pass. Nobody likes flashing blue lights in their rear-view mirror.

The northern edge of the Garrison County line was roughly fifty miles from the Canadian border. The road block would be set up on a straight stretch of Route 3 with a steep drop-off to a trout stream on one side and a sheer rock face on the other. The fugitives would be trapped.

By now, the fugitives would have fled the flatlands around Plattsburgh and Milford and climbed higher into the foothills. The serpentine road would slow them down some but it still wouldn't take long for the fleeing vehicle to reach Stone's jurisdiction.

Stone put his cellphone on speaker and called Chandler. The Mountie answered on the first ring.

"Chandler."

"It's Stone. We've got a roadblock set up on my county line. What's your location?"

"We're rolling hot, about fifteen miles from the Garrison County line, right on their tail. Two perps in a gray van, blacked out windows, New York license plate Kilo-Golf-Hotel-one-one-three. Use caution, cowboy. We think these sons of bitches are packing heat."

"Copy that. We'll be ready."

"See you soon."

Stone hung up and concentrated on driving. Minutes later, he saw the flashing lights of the roadblock up ahead. The deputies' cruisers were arranged across both lanes; with the stream drop-off on one side and the granite cliff on the other, there was no way for the incoming van to maneuver around them without crashing.

And if they were foolish or desperate enough to try, so be it. Wouldn't be the first time Stone had dragged bad guys out of a burning car wreck. He had a particularly vivid memory of a gruesome incident on the German autobahn. Not even the most zealot terrorist walks away from flipping their getaway car at 130 mph. The vehicle had been a crushed, mangled mess. The same could be said of the terrorist.

Stone pulled the Blazer in behind the staged cruisers and climbed out. He left the engine running and his emergency lights pulsing. He watched as two of his deputies deployed a spike strip a hundred yards in front of the blockade and then retreated behind their cruisers, brandishing AR-15 rifles. Valentine was already positioned behind his car, rifle braced across the roof to steady his shooting if it came to that.

Stone walked over to them. "Here's the sit-rep. We've got two guys in a gray van that jumped the border heading our way with a whole bunch of cops on their ass. They're considered armed and dangerous, so don't take any chances."

The deputies all nodded, faces grim.

"The spike strip should slow them down and hopefully they'll just give up and that'll be the end of it. But if you see a weapon pointed in our direction, light 'em up. If somebody has to die here today, make sure it's not one of us. Got it?"

More affirmative nods from the deputies. Sanchez, a recent addition to the department, even snapped out a crisp, "Yes, sir!" She was an ex-Marine and could be gung-ho as hell, especially in adrenalized situations. But she was smart, level-headed, and got the job done. So far she was fitting in nicely.

Sirens swarmed in the distance, coming closer. It was almost game time.

Stone took up position next to Valentine. Red and blue flashing lights became visible up ahead, in hot pursuit of the fugitives. The gray van swerved back and forth across both lanes like a crazy drunk to keep anyone from getting around them.

They had to know they were fighting a losing battle but refused to just give up. Stone had seen it hundreds of times before. It was some kind of felon's creed: while there is still freedom, there is still hope, however desperate.

"Lock and load," Stone muttered, talking to himself more than giving an order. He switched off the safety on his AR-15 and heard the metallic clicks as his deputies did the same.

The suspect vehicle and its convoy of pursuers rushed closer. The chase vehicles were spread out behind the van like a pack of wolves closing in on their prey, forcing it into Stone's trap.

The van slowed down as it approached the roadblock. Stone looked through the Aimpoint scope on his rifle and centered the red dot on the windshield, ready to tag-and-bag any threat he saw. If he'd been alone, he probably would have fired a warning shot, but that wouldn't fly with the feds.

The van's speed lessened even more, slowing to a crawl. Stone narrowed his eyes, barely able to make out the driver and whoever was riding shotgun. They were both gesturing wildly, probably debating what to do about the roadblock. Or maybe they had spotted the spike strip and now realized they were pretty much screwed. The pack of pursuing vehicle bunched up behind the van, cutting off any chance of retreat.

The van suddenly lurched forward, ready to run over the spike strip and ram the cruisers blocking the road. The passenger side window slid down and an arm snaked out, gripping a MAC-10. With its wicked fast cyclic rate, Stone knew the stubby machine pistol could unleash thirty .45-caliber bullets in less than two seconds. That was a whole lot of high-velocity devastation in a short amount of time.

The MAC-10 swung toward Stone and his deputies.

The threat clearly identified, Stone didn't hesitate. He never did when killing time came. He drilled a double-tap through the passenger side of the windshield. The gunman jerked in his seat as the bullets ripped through his head. The MAC-10 dropped from instantly-dead fingers and clattered onto the asphalt as blood splattered the spider-webbed glass.

The van braked to a sharp, shuddering halt.

The pursuing cars screeched to a stop behind it. Doors flew open and within seconds, there were a whole lot of weapons aimed at the idling van. Tempers were hot, adrenaline was high, and trigger fingers were itchy. It wouldn't take much of a spark for them to turn the van into a kill-box.

"You can still walk away from this!" Stone called out to the van driver. "Open the door and come out, hands up, nice and easy."

Nothing happened, the driver clearly not ready to admit defeat, even when sitting next to his shot-dead partner and surrounded by heavily-armed law enforcement agents. Stone wondered what the hell the guy was thinking. He was either going out of here with handcuffs on his wrists or bullet holes in his body. Didn't seem like a hard choice to make.

Despite the swarm of cop cars and agents, an eerie stillness seemed to grip the scene. Stone knew it well—the weird, almost ghostly calm that sometimes falls over a warzone. It settled like a wet blanket over everything, dulling some noises, amplifying others, ratcheting up the tension and the grim threat of violence. Stone could hear his own heartbeat, the adrenalized blood thundering hot through his veins.

He was just getting ready to call out to the driver again when the van door opened, the sound abnormally loud in the strange stillness. The tension cranked up another notch. Stone had no doubt that more than one trigger was now at half-pull.

"Don't do anything stupid," Stone muttered, not quite sure if he was talking to the driver or the officers surrounding him.

After several long, uncertain moments, the driver slowly emerged with his hands raised and Stone breathed a little easier. The suspect, a skinny, ragged guy in his twenties with stringy hair, stepped out onto the road, arms high like he was clutching for the clouds and a resigned look on his face. He stepped away from the van and dropped to his knees without being told. Probably not his first arrest.

US Border Patrol agents conducted the actual take-down. One hit him from behind, knocking him face-first into the concrete, while another cuffed him up. Other law enforcement personnel rushed into the van to clear it as the driver was yanked to his feet and hauled away.

Stone felt the tension ease from his muscles. He put the AR-15 on safe and slung the rifle over his shoulder. Knowing that the Border Patrol and RCMP would take it from here, he thanked his deputies for a job well done and sent them back out on patrol.

One of the agents drove the van to the side of the road. He didn't seem too fazed by the dead man in the passenger seat. A small operations area was cordoned off with orange emergency cones that left one lane open for traffic to flow around the scene, competently directed by a state trooper.

"Nice shot." Captain Chandler wandered over and stood by Stone. His white RCMP cruiser stood out like a speck of snow against the darker vehicles of the Border Patrol and State Police. "Double-tapped that moose-fucker right in the face through a windshield from over a hundred yards out. That's some damn impressive shooting."

"Just got lucky, I guess."

"Yeah, okay." Chandler snorted to show that he wasn't buying Stone's attempt to downplay the shot. "I know cowboy shit when I see it."

Stone wasn't keen on talking about his warrior past, so he quickly changed the subject. "What's the story with these guys?"

"Drug runners. We expect to find a stash somewhere in the van. Toronto PD has been surveilling them for a while now and the last few months they've been scurrying back and forth across the border more frequently than before. Made us suspicious so we decided to crash their party."

They walked over to the van, which was being guarded by a Border Patrol agent. With the feds involved, Stone feared he might run into some jurisdictional static. But the agent didn't seem interested in playing the whose-dick-is-bigger game.

"Van's clear of occupants and weapons," the agent said. "We're just getting the body out—nice shooting, by the way, sheriff—and then one of the state boys happens to be a K-9 unit, so he agreed to run the dog through there, see what he can sniff out." The agent shook his head. "I guess the dog's name is Garfield, if you can believe that shit."

"Garfield?" Chandler smirked. "They named a badass, drug-sniffing dog after a cartoon cat?"

A few minutes later, a state trooper showed up guiding one of the biggest German Shepherds Stone had ever seen. The dog whined eagerly, ready to do his job, but maintained good leash discipline.

Stone nodded at the handler. The man's nametag said 'V. HESTON.'

The Border Patrol agent opened the back door of the van. It was full of junk. "Thanks for the assist."

"No problem," said Heston. He maneuvered Garfield to the back bumper of the van and put him in a sit-stay position. Then he unleashed the Shepherd, stepped back, and said, "*Suchen!*"

The dog immediately bolted into the van.

"That's German, right?" Stone asked.

Heston nodded. "It means 'seek.' Garfield was trained

by a firm in Germany, so I had to take a crash course in the language."

"The only German I know is *wiener schnitzel*," Chandler said with a chuckle.

Stone watched as the Shepherd picked his way through the van's cluttered interior, intent on his work. Twenty seconds later, the dog stopped, let out two sharp, loud barks, and sat down next to the spare tire mounted against the wall.

"Got a hit," said Heston. He climbed into the van and rubbed the dog's head. "Good boy."

Stone stayed outside, looking in at all the junk strewn across the van's cargo space. The vehicle had apparently doubled as somebody's flop. A mattress with stuffing leaking from its burst-open side huddled in the corner. Porno mags, empty food wrappers, pizza boxes, and beer cans carpeted the floor.

Heston reached into the spare tire and pulled out a softball-sized baggie crammed full of milky white crystals. "Looks like we got ourselves some meth."

"Bingo." Chandler nodded. "Just what we suspected."

Stone pointed at the paraphernalia strewn around amidst the trash. Arm-ties, charred cook tins, used needles...the works. "Somebody's been drugging it up in here, that's for sure."

"Can't believe he ran the border with all this crap floating around." Chandler kicked at the junk. "He was either scared or desperate."

"Both, I'm guessing," Stone said, spotting a hexagonal plate with a distinctive "B" on a half-shell logo laying in the middle of the detritus like a diamond in a dung heap.

What the hell were a couple of dirtbag drug runners doing with a Bloo plate in the back of their flop van?

NINE

STONE SAT beside Cynthia Gunther's casket in the darkened church. Soon he would switch on the lights and open the doors to admit parishioners for the funeral service. But for now he sat on the top step of the altar platform, alone with Cynthia's mortal remains and his own solemn thoughts.

He reached out and rested his hand on the casket, head bowed in sorrow. The wood felt cool beneath his palm. "You're with the angels now," he whispered. "Say hello to my baby girl for me. Her name was Jasmine."

Stone felt the loss of Cynthia keenly. She had been one of his biggest supporters. His stepping behind the pulpit here at Faith Bible Church had not been without controversy, much of it stirred up by David White. But Cynthia had refused to let White's little games interfere with Stone's ministry here in Whisper Falls. She had always been unwavering in defending him to the naysayers that occasionally cropped up.

She had been a truly decent soul and he was determined to give her a dignified send-off. He silently prayed that the right words would come to him during the service.

Stone had offered to accompany Vince to the cremation after the service and he had accepted with a barely perceptible nod. The widower was grieving strangely, but clearly he didn't want to face the fire alone.

Stone knew from personal experience that even the strongest hearts have a hard time watching their loved ones turned to ash by purifying flames. He had nearly fallen to his knees while he watched his daughter's tiny coffin go into the crematorium and he was sure his sobs must have shaken the very foundation of Heaven.

A day he would never forget. Just like Vince Gunther would never forget this one.

Stone rose and walked down the aisle to the church door. He turned on the lights before unlocking and opening up. Outside, a cold breeze kicked a dead leaf across the parking lot beneath a gunmetal-gray sky. Stone stared up at the clouds and wondered if it would snow before the day ended. Some of the taller mountain peaks in the region were already capped with white.

He waited by the door until a hearse arrived, driven by Edgar Julian. The eccentric funeral director parked next to the church sign, exited the long, black car, and climbed up the front steps where Stone greeted him. David White showed up a few minutes later.

Stone said, "Dave, would you please show Mr. Julian the order of service and get him set? Thanks."

"Of course." For once, White didn't argue, proof that there was a God and miracles still happened. The two men walked down the aisle toward the casket, speaking in quiet tones.

Vince Gunther arrived a short time later. He was unsteady on his feet, like he'd maybe had one drink too many to ease his grief and soothe his nerves. He walked with his head down, as if the cold, hard gravel of the parking lot held whatever answers he sought. He wore the same dark blue suit he always wore for Sunday services, but it was more rumpled and wrinkled than usual.

He nodded to Stone as he walked up the steps, shoulders hunched as if he bore the weight of the world upon them. And hell, maybe he did. At least, the weight of *his* whole world, which had come crashing down around him.

Stone reached out and put a hand on his shoulder. "How you holding up, Vince?"

Gunther shrugged and shuffled his feet. His dress shoes were not polished. "I'm fine."

I don't believe you, Stone thought, but kept it to himself. "After the service, I'll go with you to say goodbye to Cynthia."

"Works for me," said Gunther, then ambled inside to take a seat in the front pew.

Soon the church began to fill up with mourners coming to pay their respects. One of the last to arrive was the widow Unser. She paused next to Stone, peering inside at the people gathered in the chapel. "Looks like a right proper turnout," she said.

Stone started to reply, then realized the widow wasn't paying any attention to him. She was staring intently at the back of Vince Gunther's head. Her facial expression was difficult to read. There was sympathy there, sure, but it was overshadowed by what looked like curiosity and suspicion.

For the last year or so, the two of them just stopped talking to each other. So very sad.

Stone was all too familiar with the pain of broken marriages. His own had crumbled after the death of their daughter, two grieving parents unable to find solace in each other, instead drifting apart until there was nothing left. But it sounded like the Gunthers' marriage had been broken even while they both lived in the same house.

First a broken marriage, now a broken heart.

Then again, given Vince Gunther's strange demeanor lately, maybe his heart wasn't so broken after all.

———

Two hours later, Stone stood beside Vince in the small crematorium behind the Good Fortune Funeral Home. At Vince's request, the church service had been a short, simple affair. Now it was time for Vince to say goodbye to his wife one last time.

Cynthia's casket rested on the stainless steel rollers outside the door of the cremation chamber. Edgar Julian stood off to one side, waiting patiently, giving Vince all the time he needed before the process commenced.

Turned out Vince didn't need much time at all.

"Any last words you want to say to her?" Stone asked.

Vince shook his head. "She's dead. Nothing left to say." He thrust his chin at the Bible in Stone's hands. "Go ahead and pick a verse to read and let's get this over with."

It seemed like a damned cold response but Stone wasn't here to judge how the man handled his grief. He opened his Bible to the book of John and read aloud.

"Jesus said to her, 'I am the resurrection and the life. Whoever believes in me, though he die, yet shall he live.'"

He closed the Bible and nodded to Julian. The funeral director stepped forward and opened the door to the crematory, then gently pushed the coffin inside the chamber. Stone hadn't really noticed it until now, but soft, soothing music played from hidden speakers.

Julian swung the door closed. He offered to let Vince press the button that would start the cremation process, but the widower declined. Julian did it himself, summoning the 1,800 degree flames that would reduce Cynthia Gunther's earthly body to ash. Stone found comfort in the fact that those flames could not touch her soul, which he believed was in a far better place.

He glanced over at Vince to see if the widower needed support at this difficult moment. But Vince just stared impassively at the crematory. He didn't seem to need any support.

He didn't seem to need anything at all.

———

An uneasy feeling remained with Stone as he finished up his pastoral duties and headed home. Funerals were always emotionally draining and he needed to rest and recharge. He kicked off his boots, let Max out to sniff around the property and take care of his business, and then dumped himself into the recliner with a deep sigh.

He tried not to think about Cynthia. She had been a friend and her loss hurt. And he didn't want to think about Vince and his odd behavior lately. Hell, he didn't want to think about *anything*.

He leaned back and closed his eyes. Just a few minutes, that's all he needed.

The dream snatched him almost immediately.

———

Stone stood in the small crematorium, but now it was a decrepit, desolate place. The paint peeled from the walls and Spanish moss hung from the ceiling like desiccated veils. Cynthia Gunther's casket still rested on the rollers outside the cremation chamber, but now the wood was black and rotting and swarmed with chittering bugs.

Stone tried to move, to get away from this unpleasant room, but found his feet were nailed to the floor with rusted railroad spikes that reminded him of crucifixion nails. But there was no blood and no pain. Stone found that very strange.

For a single heartbeat, Ernest Julian was there, standing beside the coffin like a tall, gaunt Grim Reaper. A crow perched on his head, beak full of maggoty meat, while the funeral director smiled despite his hollow, blown-out eye sockets. He held a primitive hammer in one hand and a silver cross in the other. His blackened fingertips looked scorched by fire.

And then another heartbeat, another tick of the clock, and Julian was gone, leaving Stone all alone. But now the room changed, transforming from a crypt-like crematorium into a deserted carnival midway. To Stone's left was a House of Mirrors; to his right, a cotton candy booth selling cobwebs wrapped around human femurs.

Straight ahead, Cynthia Gunther's casket still rested on steel rollers outside the crematory doors. The fire wasn't on yet but smoke still roiled around like a fog bank creeping in. A neon sign above the cremation chamber flashed the words FREE ASH for all the world to see in stark red letters that glowed like demon eyes.

Stone's heart pounded, his chest constricting, as if an invisible fist was trying to squeeze the life right out of him.

Something was wrong.

He sensed it.

That wasn't Cynthia in the coffin.

The public address system on the midway came to life

with a horrible noise that sounded like a giant insect clicking its jaws. A woman spoke with a sultry French accent.

"Attention! Attention! Paging Lucas Stone. Is the sheriff here or is he out looking for a horse to screw while his daughter dies?"

Panic flooded through Stone as he looked up at speaker mounted on a wooden pole. He recognized Yvonne Brossard's voice. Bloo plates dangled from the speaker like wind chimes.

"There he is! Look, everybody! See him? He's just standing there like a deer in the headlights, staring into the abyss of his own emotional trauma."

As the echo of the words died away, the voice was replaced by the sound of a celestial choir singing, except in a minor, dirge-like key. The melody was dark and underscored by the distorted growl of down-tuned guitars. Buried deep in the sonic hellscape, devils screamed and skittered.

On its own, as if pushed by an invisible, ghostly force, the casket started rolling toward the crematory. Stone's eyes widened as the chamber doors opened without the aid of human hands and the flames roared to life like a dragon's throat.

"Are you done now, Stone?" Yvonne's voice boomed from the PA system again. "Are you done feeling sorry for yourself?"

Something wasn't right.

Stone could feel it.

The coffin.

He heard the frantic thumps of someone beating on the lid…from the inside.

Someone still alive.

His daughter.

Stone screamed her name. "Jasmine!"

The casket rumbled toward the flames. *No!* He had to stop it! He lunged forward and managed to tear his feet free from the nails, leaving them marked like stigmata. But the air suddenly seemed to be the consistency of gelatin, slowing him down. Phantasmal, skeletal hands seemed to clutch at him, dragging him backwards.

Yvonne's voice again. "Paging Sheriff Stone! Better put that fire out before it hurts somebody you love!"

The coffin picked up speed. The rollers had lengthened, now impossibly long, like the unending corridor of an ancient castle. The flames roared like the very fires of Hell itself, hungry to unleash fiery damnation.

The lid suddenly blew off as if there had been a volcanic eruption inside the casket. For one terrible heartbeat, Stone expected to see his daughter crawling out in a black cloud of death and decay.

Instead, he woke up with a shuddering shout.

———

Stone jerked awake in the recliner, breath heaving in ragged gasps, cold sweat beading his brow. A quick glance at the clock revealed he'd been asleep for less than fifteen minutes. Not very long, but long enough for the vivid nightmare to sneak up and ambush his subconscious.

Max was sitting at his feet, scarred head cocked to the side in a quizzical look that seemed to say, *You all right, man?*

Shaking his own head to get rid of the last vestiges of the all-too-vivid dream, Stone reached down and rubbed the Shottie between the ears. "All good, buddy. No worries."

He climbed out of the chair, went to the kitchen sink, and splashed some cold water on his face. He could feel his stress level start to recede. He wasn't one to look for signs and symbols in dreams, so he didn't bother psycho-analyzing the ghastly images his slumbering brain had conjured up. He took several deep breaths until his heart stopped pounding in his chest.

He dried his face with a hand towel, picked up his cellphone, and called his favorite person.

Holly answered on the second ring. "Hi."

"Am I calling at a bad time?"

"It's never a bad time when you call." Stone could practically feel her smile through the phone. "What's up?"

Stone stared out the window, the dream still fresh in his mind. "Think I need a drink. Care to join me?"

"Sure, I'd love to."

"Meet me at the usual place."

———

Located on Main Street just two blocks up from the sheriff's station, the Jack Lumber Bar was the favorite watering hole of Whisper Fall natives. The tourists tended to stick to the fancier hotel bars or trendy micro-breweries, and the college kids typically headed to Lake Placid or Plattsburgh to hit a nightclub, leaving the Jack Lumber for locals just looking for a low-key, kick-back-and-relax joint. Exactly Stone's kind of place.

The Jack Lumber was a long, narrow room with a bar on one side and a series of small booths on the other. These ran parallel toward the jukebox that cranked out the music for the small dance floor in the back. All the times Stone had been in here, he had never once seen anyone actually dancing, even though the juke usually kept up a steady flow of classic rock tunes.

Stone walked in and greeted Griz, owner of the place

and the only man allowed behind the bar. "Hey, Griz. How's it going?"

"I'm still above ground, so I'm doing fine, thanks. Good to see you, sheriff." A quiet, 75-year-old black man, Skip 'Grizzle' Travers served as something of a sage around Whisper Falls—a drink-slinging philosopher who minded his roost with fatherly protectiveness and no shortage of wisdom gained from a long, observant life. Some people visited the Jack Lumber for advice just as much as they came for the booze.

Grizzle flipped a coaster in front of Stone as he took a seat at the bar. "You come here to drink, jaw-jack, or looking for information?"

"Just a drink. Meeting Holly here."

"Another date, huh?"

"We've been over this, Griz. We're just friends."

Grizzle snorted. "Yeah, you just go ahead and keep telling yourself that, preacher."

Stone pointedly ignored him until Holly arrived. "Just friends" or not, Stone had to admit she looked real damn good walking through the door, her brown hair pulled into a short ponytail, her electric-blue eyes gleaming warmly when she saw him. She wore black jeans that hugged her lower curves and a red sweater that concealed her upper ones. A large silver cross dangled around her neck.

She slid onto the stool next to him. "This seat taken?"

"It is now."

"I'm glad you called. Heck of a day at the diner. I could use a drink."

"You and me both."

Grizzle wandered over. "What can I get you two lovebirds?"

Holly said, "We're just friends, Griz."

The bartender rolled his eyes so hard he probably saw

the back of his skull. "You two practice that line together before you wandered in here?"

Holly ordered a glass of white wine. Grizzle rustled it up, along with a Jack and Coke, lots of ice, easy on the Jack for Stone. Another couple sat at a high-top table in the back of the bar, snacking on a shared pile of cheesy fries while giving each other looks that hinted they couldn't wait to get home and snack on each other. Other than that, the place was empty.

Holly sipped her wine. "How was the funeral?"

"Fine, I guess." Stone swilled the cola-whiskey mix in his glass, causing the ice to rattle against the sides. "Vince just seemed off. Like he wasn't really there."

"Grief hits people in different ways," she said.

"You talking about Vince Gunther?" Grizzle paused from polishing a glass. "The man's been in here steady, almost every day for the past month or so."

"Really?" The news surprised Stone. "I've never seen him."

"Neither have I," said Holly.

"He's a day drinker," Grizzle explained. "Comes in around noon, gets tanked up real good, and then heads back home. Started hitting it heavy about a month ago. Probably be even worse now that Cynthia died."

Interesting, thought Stone.

"Where's he been staying since the fire?" Holly asked.

"One of the local real estate agents is a member of the church," Stone replied. "He put Vince up in one of his apartments."

"Henry Hutt, right? That's the real estate guy?"

"Yeah. You know him?"

"He's the one providing housing for Lizzie's friend, Luisa Valdez, and her family. He's been really good to them."

"Hutt's one of the good guys. Not a greedy bastard like some people in his profession."

"Gonna be tough on Vince, living alone after being married all those years," Grizzle remarked.

"Sure is." Holly glanced at Stone. "Life is better when you can share it with someone."

Stone locked eyes with her for a long moment and a lot went unspoken between them in those few seconds. Too many wounds in their pasts for either of them to fully open their hearts again.

Just friends, dammit.

Stone's cellphone buzzed, interrupting whatever stolen moment they were having. Feeling both relief and regret, he answered. "This is Stone."

"Sheriff, it's Valentine. We've got ourselves another fire."

TEN

STONE DROVE down Wildflower Avenue to the other end of town. Even if he had not been given the address, the pulsing lights and column of gray smoke smudging the November night sky would have let him know where to go: Crescent Self Storage Facility.

The business was located behind a tow-truck company, a string of storage units tucked back in a cluster of blue spruce trees. The sheriff's department even leased a couple units to store their archived files and old evidence.

Based on the single tower of smoke—as opposed to roiling clouds of it—it looked to be a smaller blaze. As Stone rolled up on the scene, he wondered if it was an accident or another deliberate burn. One thing he knew for sure—he was getting sick of fires.

He parked along the chain-link fence that surrounded the storage facility, which was constructed from cinderblock. He spotted flames blossoming from a unit at the end of the row. He circled around to the gate, which was currently being guarded by Cade Valentine.

"Fire chief is down there." The deputy pointed in the

general direction of the blaze. "He's been looking for you." Valentine seemed unusually cheerful.

"What's up with you?" Stone asked. "We've got another burn and you're all smiles."

"Oh, nothing." Valentine smiled mysteriously. "Just thinking about my plans for later."

"Those plans involve Yvonne Brossard?"

The deputy didn't respond but the shit-eating grin on his face said it all.

Stone smirked and said, "Careful with that hellcat. She might just rip you to ribbons."

"Maybe. But God, what a way to go."

Shaking his head, Stone headed down the concrete row, stepping over the fire hoses that snaked across the ground. The emergency lights of the firetrucks scoured him with flashes of red and blue, his Stetson throwing his face into shadow.

Stone followed the hoses until he found Dennis Fox standing outside a unit marked D-6, supervising the crew.

"Got the coroner's report," the fire chief said without preamble. "We should sit down and talk about it."

"Stop by the office tomorrow morning."

"That'll work." Fox jerked his chin toward the smoking, water-drenched storage unit. "This is my bowling league night. Call came in and I hustled over right from the lanes. Five more strikes and I would've had a perfect game."

"The sacrifices we make for the job."

"You said it. Maybe it's time to retire."

They waited for the smoke to clear and the scene to cool down enough to have a look around. Once they were good to go, Fox led the way into the unit.

"These things usually only burn for one reason," the fire chief said.

"And what would that reason be?" Stone asked.

The chief looked unhappy as he shined his flashlight on a charred mattress in the corner. "Because somebody's living in them."

Stone knew it happened. It was illegal, sure, but legalities didn't matter much to people who had nowhere else to go.

"Looks like someone was camped out in here." Fox kicked at the mattress.

"They were doing more than camping." Stone's flashlight beam fell on what looked like a jerry-rigged chemistry set arranged on a side table.

Fox let out a low whistle. "Damn. You thinking meth?"

That was exactly what Stone was thinking, but he didn't reply. He was too busy staring at a hexagonal container sitting on the table next to a glass beaker. He didn't need to turn it over to know that there was a distinctive "B on a half-shell" logo on the bottom.

————

Dennis Fox showed up at the sheriff's station the next morning with two coffees from the quaint little café up the street. He settled into a chair across from Stone and dropped four files on his desk.

"Those are the preliminary reports on our fires." He fanned the files out like a deck of cards. "The Gunther burn, the RV burn, the old hunting shack last week, and now last night's burn."

Stone drained half his coffee in a single shot. He needed a fast caffeine injection. He hadn't slept much last night and was feeling it this morning. "That's a lot of fires in a short stretch of time."

"I can spare you all the technical details," Fox said.

"It's all in the files if you want to read them later and put yourself to sleep. But between our investigation and the coroner's report on Cynthia Gunther, we're starting to piece together what we think we're dealing with here."

"I'm listening."

Fox unbuttoned his coat and leaned back in the chair. "All four burns had one thing in common—chemical accelerant. We haven't pinpointed the exact cause of the fires yet, but all of them were given a boost by an accelerant. We found traces at each of the sites."

"What kind of chemical accelerant?" Stone asked.

"Good old-fashioned lighter fluid."

"Simple but effective," Stone said. "So we've got an arsonist who likes to keep things low-tech."

"Looks that way," Fox agreed.

"Not sure that helps us much. Lighter fluid is pretty common."

"Sold in eight stores in Whisper Falls alone." Fox sighed. "Probably a hundred sales in just the path couple of months. Waste of time digging through receipts or store security footage."

"You also have to take into account that it could have been purchased out of town," Stone said.

"Exactly. There's just no way of knowing." Fox shook his head and his expression turned grim. "But one thing's for sure, we've got ourselves a goddamned fire-freak right here in Garrison County. And they're picking up steam."

ELEVEN

YVONNE BROSSARD STOOD at the window wearing nothing but a silk robe, hair still wet from the shower-for-two she and Mason had recently enjoyed, and watched Mason Xavier's helicopter rise from the landing pad outside his mansion. It hovered in the air like a dragonfly for a few moments and then banked south, heading for Albany. Probably for some kind of boring business meeting that started with caviar and ended with champagne.

Once the chopper vanished from sight, she dug a pack of cigarettes out of her purse and fired one up. She took a long, appreciative drag and thought it tasted like freedom.

Mason didn't like her to smoke in the house. But he would be gone for the next two or three days so she had the place to herself. Thank God for small favors.

She liked Mason, and they got along well, both in and out of bed, but she was the kind of woman who thrived on her own sovereignty. When in Mason's company, she was expected to defer to him, sort of an unspoken agreement between them. But when she was alone, it was a different story.

She finished her cigarette, stubbing it out in a Bloo ashtray that cost enough to feed a small family for a week, and then sent a text on her cellphone. That task completed, she dropped the phone into the pocket of her robe, picked up the ashtray, and sauntered into the kitchen.

She considered ditching the robe and strolling around in the nude, but company was on the way. Then again, Darius had seen her naked plenty of times. She settled for untying the robe and letting it hang open. Let him have glimpses of the goods instead of the full show.

A large window allowed her to look west and see the driveway as it swept up to the house. Yvonne settled down at the counter and smoked contentedly for the next ten minutes, finishing two more cigarettes. As she stabbed the second one into the ashtray, a low-slung, black sports car—a Lotus Evora GT—pulled up beside the house. She knew what it was because she had bought it for him.

Yeah, sovereignty was good. But control was even better.

Darius, a slender, unshaven, olive-skinned man, uncoiled himself from the driver's seat, his expression impassive behind a pair of mirrored aviator shades. He wore a black leather jacket silver-streaked with zippers. He stretched as if to ease the muscle kinks from a long drive, then pivoted on his square-toed boots and headed toward the house.

Yvonne met him at the door. *"Salut, ma copain,"* she greeted, kissing him on both cheeks.

"Salut, madame." Darius bowed slightly

"Come in." Yvonne continued to speak in French. Darius followed her inside, sat down beside her on one of the stools at the kitchen counter, and lit a cigarette. One of their many shared vices.

Darius looked around and exhaled smoke. "Whoever your latest guy is, he's done pretty well for himself." Like Yvonne, his French contained the Joual twang of a Quebecois. "He's a good investment, I take it?"

Yvonne shrugged. "He's got good connections."

"I'll bet he's real happy 'making a connection' with you." Darius grinned as he raked his eyes unapologetically down her exposed cleavage. He knew from personal experience how good it was to 'connect' with Yvonne Brossard. She used both sex and money to bend people to her will and he had enjoyed both along the way.

"He hasn't complained yet," Yvonne said.

"There's not a guy on this earth who is going to complain while those legs of yours are wrapped around his waist."

"Darius, Darius." Yvonne smiled and shook her head. "What am I going to do with you?"

"As long as you continue to pay me, whatever you want." Darius tapped ash. "I've got the crew on stand-by. Two here and two that I can get across the border quick if I have to. All depends on what you need."

"That remains to be seen." Yvonne's face tightened. "We've had some disruptions, production is down right now, and the local police are sticking their noses into my business."

"Noses can be broken. Hell, they can be cut off."

Her lips twisted into a cold smile. "God, I love it when you talk dirty."

Smirking, Darius rose from his seat. At the same time, Yvonne stood up and bent over the counter like some kind of wanton vixen. Darius dropped his pants, hiked the robe up over her waist, and took her right then and there.

Or more accurately, Yvonne *let* herself be taken. Like all men, Darius could be controlled with his dick. Letting him satisfy his animalistic urges kept him compliant, pliable, eating out of the palm of her hand. Besides, she was about to ask him to do something terrible and savage, so the least she could do was let him get his rocks off first.

Afterwards, when they were back sitting on their stools, Darius asked, "So what kind of production problems are you having?"

"Personality conflicts." Yvonne waved her hand dismissively. "Nothing that I can't handle on my end."

"Making the machine run smoothly is the challenge of management," Darius said. "That's why you make the big bucks."

"You get paid well, too." Yvonne narrowed her eyes at him. "And when things go wrong on *your* end, you have to answer for them."

"Is there a problem?"

Yvonne drummed her nails on the countertop. "One of our shipments deviated from the plan and ended up on a back road in the woods."

"I heard."

"What went wrong?"

"Not sure." Darius shrugged. "It was one of the new drivers, that foreigner we hired. He needed money, we waved a wad of cash under his nose, and he agreed to take the job. But he failed to deliver. I'm not even sure if he picked up the shipment."

"Oh, the shipment got picked up, all right," Yvonne said. "By the police. This town has got a real, live Wyatt Earp here. Wears a cowboy hat and everything. He hooked up with the RCMP and the product is in their hands now."

Darius considered this news in silence, then finally said, "That's not good."

"Damn right it's not good," Yvonne said. "And it's your mess to clean up. We can't have our couriers blowing off and abandoning their shipments. I trust you see the problem here?"

Darius nodded.

"You need to send a message to the other drivers. Maintain discipline in the ranks. They need to remember who they're working for. Am I clear?"

"Yeah, I got it." Darius managed to keep his tone both annoyed and respectful. Ten minutes ago he'd enjoying all the pleasures her body had to offer. Now the master was reminding him that the pleasure came with a price.

Yvonne handed him a slip of paper. "That's the name and address of the courier and his family. Send a message and make sure it's loud and clear. No more mistakes."

Darius asked, "What about the sheriff?"

"I'll deal with the sheriff." Yvonne's eyes glinted dangerously as she thought about the cowboy and what she would do to him. "You just make sure that courier knows he fucked up."

————

Luisa Valdez' legs ached as she biked home from her friend Lizzy's house. She had stayed longer than expected and now dusk had fallen and covered the world with blue-black shadows like ink blots. Lizzy's mom, Holly, had offered to drive her home, but Luisa had declined. She only lived a few miles up the road, she enjoyed bike-riding, and accepting charity from others always made her uncomfortable for some reason.

Since she and her parents had been placed in Garrison County as part of a refugee worker program, the three of them struggled to make ends meet. They all pitched in to work and help the family remain afloat, and they stubbornly refused handouts. It was a matter of pride with them. Of course it wasn't easy but it was worth it to be in America. There had been nothing but misery for them back in the Honduras.

Luisa worked every day after school washing dishes at the small café attached to the regional airport, doing her best not to talk too much, embarrassed by her heavily-accented English. Her mother cleaned rooms at a motel in Tupper Lake. Her father...

Well, actually, she wasn't quite sure what her father did for money. He got fidgety when she asked about it and mumbled something about "doing some things for some people," whatever that meant. But he had come home the other night with cash in his pocket, so he was doing *something*.

She was a quarter-mile from home when a black sports car with no headlights on pulled out of a side road and clipped the front tire of her bike. She went flying, landing hard on her back, the breath knocked out of her. The ground beneath her felt cold and unforgiving.

Fear quivered through her as the car braked to a halt, taillights flashing red in the near-dark of dusk. The driver emerged, little more than a shadow in the twilight.

Luisa felt her fight-or-flight response kicking in, but she was too disoriented the fall to make a choice. And so the choice was made for her.

The man rushed over and seized her, one hand gripping her upper arm like a vice, cruel fingers digging deep and bruising bone. The other hand wagged an ugly black pistol in her face.

"Come with me and I won't kill your parents," the man hissed.

My parents? Fresh fear crept into her veins. What was

he planning on doing to her parents? She had no way of knowing whether or not he was bluffing, but she couldn't take the risk. She needed to do everything in her power to protect them.

So when he yanked her to her feet and shoved her toward the car, she went obediently, without a fight. She didn't even bother yelling for help; there was no one around to hear her. Nor did she fight when he used metal zip-ties to secure her wrists, not even when they cut deep into her skin. Instead, she went into a sort of self-induced daze.

It was something she had taught herself to do when things got unpleasant. Growing up poor in Honduras, she'd had plenty of practice. She could just mentally check out at will, fog her brain, go somewhere else. She was very good at it.

She remained in this trance as the black sports car raced out of town and into a familiar part of the forest. The brain-fog did not lift even when her abductor parked on the side of a dirt road and dragged her into the trees. A small corner of her mind, still switched on, still aware on a subconscious level, recognized the burned-down hunting shack she and Lizzy had discovered a couple weeks ago.

But the rest of her dreamed of her former country, her old home, the grandmother who cooked the best meals of anyone on earth.

Then the dream turned into a nightmare when the man wearing a jacket full of zippers produced a can of lighter fluid and doused her with it. Her protective trance evaporated as she felt the flammable liquid soak her hair and clothes.

He pulled a box of wooden matches out of his jacket pocket and dragged one along the striker strip. It flared to life and drove the shadows from his face, revealing a cold, shark-like smile. "Sorry, *senorita*," he said, not sounding sorry at all. "But sometimes children pay for the sins of their father."

Luisa didn't understand what he meant, but that didn't matter. Nothing mattered at all except what was about to happen.

He tossed the match and the flames engulfed her within seconds. Her agonized screams lasted a whole lot longer than that as the flesh melted from her bones. But only the man and God could hear her and both just watched her burn in silence.

TWELVE

"SO WHAT DO you think his reason is?" Stone looked across the table at Dennis Fox. The Birch Bark Diner was quiet mid-morning, the early breakfast eaters having shuffled off to their 9-to-5 jobs while the lunch crowd still had a couple more hours left before they showed up. Which meant he and Fox pretty much had the place to themselves. He had thought Holly was working but she was nowhere to be found.

"Hard to say." Fox sipped his coffee. A half-eaten bowl of maple-flavored oatmeal rested on the table near his elbow.

"Maybe it's a 'her.'" Stone let the thought hang there.

"Oh, it's a male," Fox said. "I'd bet good money on it."

"What makes you so sure?"

"Pyromaniacs are almost always male," Fox replied. "Female arsonists are relatively rare. The odds are three to one that our fire-freak is a guy. It's an impulse-control thing."

"Most crime is, when you get right down to it."

"Pyros are a different breed. Their brain circuits got wired wrong. They're cracked, and not just a little bit." Fox took another sip of coffee. "Or maybe it's just teenagers being stupid and blowing off steam."

"What about the drug angle?"

"It's possible," said Fox. "But how does the Gunther home fit into that?"

"It doesn't," Stone admitted.

When the waitress, an older woman named Emily, wandered over to top off their coffee, Stone asked her if she had seen Holly.

"She was here early," Emily said. "But then the school called and she had to take off in a hurry. I don't know the details, but I guess Lizzy got into some trouble."

The last syllable had barely left her mouth when Fox's cellphone chimed. The fire chief opened the text and his face hardened.

Stone's cellphone went off a few seconds later. His text was similar and his face turned equally grim.

Fox said, "Time to go."

———

Driving the Blazer, Stone led the way down the logging road. On any other day, this would be a pleasant drive. But when he spotted the line of emergency vehicles parked up ahead, he knew this outing was going to be anything but pleasant.

Stone pulled off to the side and Fox parked behind him. He spotted the burned-down remains of a hunting shack and realized this must be the shack Holly and her friend Luisa had discovered last week. Emergency personnel were gathered around something on the ground that was covered by a tarp. A short distance away, Deputy Valentine stood with Lizzy and Holly.

Stone went over to them. Lizzy sat on a moss-covered boulder, swaddled in a thick blanket. A paramedic knelt beside her, a concerned look on his face as he checked her vitals. Holly stood with one hand on her daughter's shoulder, looking stricken.

"What happened?" Stone asked.

Holly turned to him. "My God, Luke." She glanced over at the tarp on the ground and fought back tears. Despite her best efforts, one broke loose and coursed down her cheek.

Stone knelt down beside Lizzy. She stared off into space as if he wasn't there. "Liz, what happened?"

No response. She didn't move. Didn't even look at him. She seemed almost catatonic.

"She'll be okay," the paramedic said. "She's just had a really bad shock. Might take some time to process."

"Process *what*?" Stone stood up and looked at Valentine.

"Sheriff, it looks like our fire investigation has turned into a homicide investigation," Valentine said. "Lizzy here…"

"Lizzy skipped school," Holly interrupted. "She lied to me. Went off this morning just like any other day and…" Her voice trailed off as she squeezed her eyes shut and shook her head, the tears flowing freely now.

"We were supposed to meet here at the shack."

All eyes turned to Lizzy as she finally broke her silence.

"We were just going to skip school and hike around." Lizzy shivered and pulled the blanket more tightly around her shoulders. "We played hooky because Luisa never gets any free time. She always has to work."

Stone touched her shoulder. "I'm not excusing what you did," he said quietly. "But I get it."

"I found her." Lizzy acted like she didn't hear him, her voice hollow and dull. "Over there."

She lapsed into silence again. Stone waited a full half-minute for her to say something else, but it looked like Lizzy was done talking for now.

He turned and walked over to the tarp on the ground. He didn't want to subject himself to this, but it was time to have a look. It was his job and he had an obligation not to turn away from the hard stuff.

A paramedic stepped in front of him. "It's bad, sheriff. Real bad."

"I know. But I still need to see it."

The paramedic hesitated, then reached down and pulled back the tarp.

Luisa Valdez was laying on her back as if frozen in place, arms and legs curled inward toward her torso. Metal zip-ties shackled her wrists. Very little remained of her clothes and her skin was a charred wreckage. Burns covered her entire body but some parts suffered worse than others. Her face had been partially spared. Stone could make out the mottled red of what had been a mouth, open and screaming to reveal a fire-scorched throat.

Stone abruptly turned away and walked over to a nearby oak tree. He steadied himself against the trunk and took several deep breaths. He had seen too much death to feel like vomiting but the sight of this burnt girl still hit him like a sucker punch to the guts. The fact that it was Lizzy's friend made it even worse.

His daughter's face swept through his mind like a ghost, both a comfort and a haunt. He knew all too well what it felt like to watch an innocent life get snuffed out too soon.

Rage coiled in the pit of his stomach like a cold, hard knot.

He went back over to Holly and said, "Why don't you take Lizzy home? I'll come by later and talk to her."

Holly nodded, worry lines etched on her face. She helped Lizzy get up from the boulder and led her toward the line of vehicles. Lizzy shuffled along blankly, more zombie than human.

Stone returned to the tarp. Dennis Fox knelt down, picked up a corner, and peered underneath. If he experienced a gut-punch reaction, he didn't show it. His eyes were clinical as they assessed the charred corpse.

"If I had to guess, I'd say she died from the burn itself," Fox said. "Most people succumb to smoke inhalation but that doesn't look to be the case here. I'd bet dollars to dimes that somebody set this poor girl on fire deliberately."

Stone nodded, trying not to think about how horrific Luisa's death must have been, and vowing there would be justice for her killing.

———

Stone called the coroner and asked him to put a rush on his preliminary autopsy report. Somebody had burned a teenage girl alive and they needed answers ASAP, before it happened again. The coroner promised to get right on it.

Deputy Valentine rounded up the Valdezes and brought them to the sheriff's station where Stone broke the terrible news to them. This was easily the worst part of his job. The mother couldn't contain her grief and wailed loudly; her husband remained more stoic, with just a slight glistening of the eyes and a small quiver of the lip betraying the pain he felt.

They assured Stone that Luisa had not fallen in with a bad crowd. In fact, as far as they knew, Lizzy was her only friend. When she wasn't in school, she was working at the airport café. She'd had no time to get into trouble.

Yeah, well, trouble found her anyway, Stone thought grimly but kept it to himself.

Mrs. Valdez broke down again, sobbing, no longer able to speak. Stone expressed his sympathy and let them go home. By that time, the glistening in the father's eyes had turned to full-fledged tears that streamed down his face. Stone knew exactly the kind of hurt the man was feeling. Losing a daughter was not something you ever really recovered from. You just learned, somehow, to live with the pain.

———

Late that afternoon, Stone received a copy of the coroner's preliminary report in his email. Fox must have gotten his copy at the same time because he called almost immediately.

"Looks like our arsons and Luisa's murder might be connected," the fire chief said. "Luisa's killer doused her in lighter fluid and set her on fire."

"That would never hold up in court."

"If there's a God in Heaven, I pray this sick bastard never sees a courtroom, if you know what I mean."

Oh, there's a God in Heaven, Stone thought. *And there's a good chance He's going to answer your prayer. I just have to find the son of a bitch first.*

———

Stone showed up at Holly's place after dinner.

"How is she?" Stone asked, taking off his Stetson and hanging up his rancher's coat.

"She's pretty shaken up." Holly sounded worried.

"She had really bonded with Luisa and now this happens. I think she's still in shock."

In the kitchen, Lizzy sat at the table, head down, swaddled in a blanket, a glass of ginger ale in front of her. She seemed to be staring at the carbonation bubbles as they crawled up the sides of the glass. She did not look up when Stone sat down across from her.

"Hey, Lizzy."

"Hi, Luke." She spoke flatly, still not looking at him.

Stone traded a glance with Holly, then asked, "How you holding up?"

She said nothing.

"Lizzy," Holly said. "Please…"

"Fine." Lizzy slapped the table, her voice exasperated and angry. "You want to hear what I think? I'll tell you what I think. I think it's fucked up and unfair. Luisa never hurt anybody. She was just an all-around good person. That's why I liked her. Most high-school kids are royal jerks, but not her."

Stone stayed quiet, letting her talk, sensing that right now she just needed someone to listen.

"Luisa was really mature for her age. That's another reason I liked her so much." Lizzy brushed away a tear that had escaped the corner of her eye. "Most other teens just bore me most of the time. But not Luisa. She was smart, and most people didn't even realize it because she struggled with English. If people would have just taken the time to talk to her, they would have realized she'd been through a lot in her time."

"She had a hard life," Holly said quietly.

"And a hard death," said Lizzy. More tears streaked her face. "I'm going to miss her smile."

Stone reached across the table and touched her hand. "Can you tell me what happened today?"

"We were just going to skip school and spend the day

hanging out in the woods. I even packed us a couple of bag lunches. Luisa said in her country, you couldn't just go wandering in the forest because it was too dangerous. She said there were gangs hanging around that would kill you."

"Death squads," Stone said. "Been a problem down there since the '80s."

"It's one of the reasons they wanted to get out of the country. Did you know they walked most of the way here? In one of those migrant caravans. I can't even imagine." Lizzy shook her head. "Anyway, she just wanted to spend today having some fun. She works hard but her boss is a jerk, always making fun of her accent."

Hearing that made Stone want to track down Luisa's boss and punch him in the mouth until he couldn't talk right either. Some people just deserved to have their teeth knocked down their throat.

"There was some trouble at home, too," Lizzy said.

"What kind of trouble?"

"Luisa wouldn't come right out and say. Just said her dad was acting weird and her parents argued a lot. Guess it had something to do with his job but she wasn't even sure where he works right now."

Stone leaned back in his chair, mulling over the information she had given him, trying to figure out how skipping school had cost a young girl her life.

Lizzy took a sip of her soda and then abruptly asked, "Do you think she's in Heaven?"

"Luisa?"

"Yeah."

"The Bible says God loves children more than anything, so yeah, I think she's in Heaven."

"Good. Makes me want to go there even more. But Luke?"

"Yeah?"

"The bastard who did this to her? I hope they burn in Hell."

Preacher or not, Stone understood exactly how she felt.

THIRTEEN

STONE STUCK around Holly's place for another hour and then headed home. He'd been too busy to buy groceries for the past couple of weeks so he decided to stop at Sloane's Emporium and grab a few things until he could find time for a proper supply run. Whisper Falls was the kind of town where the sidewalks were mostly rolled up by 8:00 p.m. on weekdays. Sloane's was one of the rare places that stayed open later.

Stone grabbed a basket from the stack by the door. As he entered one of the aisles, he spotted Raff working, loitering around in a black hoodie, doing his best to look inconspicuous as he watched for shoplifters. He saw Stone and came over.

"Hey, sheriff. Got a second?" Raff was a short, slender, bearded man who more often than not wore a crooked grin.

"Sure, what's up?"

"Dale's in." Raff jerked his chin in the general direction of the hardware section. "He's over there loading up on flashlights and spray-paint."

Stone frowned. Dale, like Scooby, was one of Whisper

Falls' resident meth-heads and a notorious booster. "You need back-up?" he asked.

"You mind?"

"Not a bit." Stone plucked a box of cereal off the shelf and some coffee. "Heading to the cash register now."

"Perfect." Raff started heading toward the exit. "I'll wait outside and we'll nail him when he goes out. Thanks for the assist."

Stone nodded and headed toward the cashier. Raff was dedicated, no doubt about that. Loss prevention work didn't pay much but Raff was always in the game. He could have made more money working in a metropolitan area like Albany or New York City, but he preferred to ply his trade in the small mountain towns of the Adirondacks. It was a sentiment that Stone understood and respected.

"Evening, preacher." Madge, the cashier, was an elderly woman wearing a Sloane's baseball cap. "Or are you the sheriff tonight?"

"Little bit of both, Madge." Stone glanced out the window. Raff hovered on the sidewalk, just to one side of the exit.

"Well, whether you're wearing the badge or carrying a Bible, it's always good to see you." Madge gave him a grandmotherly smile, the kind of smile that should be home baking cookies, not bagging groceries. "You just make this old gal feel safe, ya know? Maybe it's the cowboy hat."

Using his peripheral vision, Stone saw Dale emerge from the hardware aisle, a backpack slung over his shoulder. The guy was trying so hard to act nonchalant that it had the exact opposite effect and made him look sketchy as hell.

Stone wondered if Dale would go for the "discount" or a straight up "rip-and-run." The discount—buying one cheap item while boosting the others—was easier. The rip-and-run saved money but was riskier, so it took some balls. Or stupidity.

Stone turned his head and glanced at Dale as he walked by. He was dressed in a black hoodie—what was it with shoplifters and black hoodies these days?—and baggy jeans. With his clean-shaven face and cue-ball scalp, Dale could have passed as a monk. But the bleary eyes, knife scar that ran down his cheek from his left ear, and the drug-induced twitchiness ruined that particular illusion.

Dale nodded to Madge, ignored Stone, and headed out the door.

Madge shook her head disapprovingly. "That man does not walk with the angels."

"Maybe the fallen kind," Stone said. "I'll be right back."

Outside, Raff had intercepted Dale. The shoplifter looked sullen, hands stuffed in the pockets of his hoodie. Stone exited the store and walked up behind them.

"...see what you've got in your backpack," Raff was saying. "We can do this the easy way, or we can..."

"Fuck you, asshole!" Dale screeched, his voice barely an octave below falsetto. "You're not a cop, you're just a fucking tin-badge wannabe. Suck my dick!"

Raff looked like he wanted to make Dale eat asphalt and boot-stomp his face until it looked like it had been run through a meat grinder. Hell, maybe he would have if Stone hadn't been there. Stone thought about walking away so Raff could take care of business and shut the man's foul mouth.

Without warning, Dale's right hand came out of his pocket brandishing a crescent wrench that he had probably just boosted from the store. He swung it at Raff's temple.

Raff brought both arms up to block, grunting as the wrench struck bone. Stone stepped forward and drove his boot into the back of Dale's knee. The limb buckled and the junkie screeched, twisted, and went down like a puppet with its strings slashed.

Raff knelt beside Dale and grabbed his right arm to restrain him. Stone was reaching for his cuffs when Dale pulled a syringe out of his left pocket and jammed it into the back of Raff's hand. The point stabbed all the way through and popped out his palm. Raff snarled in pain and instinctively let go.

Dale rolled to his feet and ran away. His high-pitched cackle floated back like an echoing taunt as his feet pounded the pavement, carrying out his escape.

He managed less than a dozen steps before Stone hit him like a wrecking ball from behind and he face-planted on the parking lot cement. The cold concrete ripped his features with road rash.

Stone put a knee between his shoulder blades, pinning him to the ground while he slapped on the cuffs. "Dumb move, Dale," he growled. "Hope you like jail food."

As Stone hauled Dale to his feet, something slipped from the junkie's hoodie pocket.

A can of lighter fluid.

———

While Raff headed over to the Adirondack Medical Center emergency room to get patched up, Stone formally arrested Dale and took him in for processing.

"This is bullshit!" Dale snarled, the scar on his face pulsing so red in anger that it matched the bloody road-rash stripes. "I didn't do nothin'!"

"Right." Stone clasped Dale's elbow in one hand

carried his backpack in the other, pushing him through the door of the sheriff's station. "You were just minding your own business. Filling your backpack with thirteen flashlights and eight cans of spray paint and walking out of Sloane's with it."

"I was gonna pay for that, but then you two ass-lickers jumped me."

"Tell it to the judge." Stone took Dale into his office and shoved him down into a chair. "But not until I ask you some questions first."

Deputy Lewis, a.k.a. "Catfish," stuck his head in. "Need any help, boss?" he asked in his Cajun-flavored drawl. He was a Louisiana transplant who had traded the bayous for the mountains. He also had a wild streak a mile wide and was a crack sniper who bragged he could "shoot the balls off a gnat at a thousand yards."

"Not yet," Stone said as he sat down behind his desk. "But if I need someone to put a bullet in his kneecap, I'll call you."

"I'm your guy. Just give a holler."

When the deputy left, Stone dumped the backpack out on his desk. He took his time stacking the stolen items in neat, orderly rows, letting Dale sweat. Finally, he set the can of lighter fluid on the edge of the desk, front and center.

"You a smoker, Dale?"

"Eat shit."

"Tell me about this." Stone tapped the can.

"It's lighter fluid." Dale shrugged. "So what?"

"You don't have any lighters on you."

"Yeah. So?"

"So lighter fluid has been used in a series of recent arsons in the county." Stone watched Dale carefully as he spoke. "Somebody likes setting things on fire." A brief pause, then: "Including a young girl."

Dale stared at him and Stone could practically hear the meth-addled gears in his head grinding away as he mulled over the information. He looked worried, then mad, then switched back to worried, before pivoting back to mad and staying there.

"Fuck you!" he fumed. "I didn't do a goddamned thing."

"Right. Innocent folks like yourself always go around jamming needles through people's hands."

"Fuck you!"

"Yeah, I heard you the first time."

Stone booked him, hitting the guy with multiple charges including theft and assault, and tossed him in a holding cell. The "fuck you" escalated as Dale added even more colorful profanities to the insult and repeated them like a broken record. Stone had to admit that some of the language combinations had a gutter-style flourish to them. If Dale turned out to be responsible for Luisa's death and Stone had to kill him, he was pretty sure the man's last words would only contain four letters.

Raff showed up a short time later, hand bandaged. "Getting ready to head home. You need a statement from me or anything?"

"It'll keep until tomorrow," Stone said. "But I did want to talk to you about something."

"No problem. Mind if we go outside so I can have a smoke?"

"Sure."

Stone followed the loss prevention specialist out to the parking lot. They stood beneath the yellow glow of a streetlamp crusted with dead bugs as Raff fished a pack of cigarettes from his pocket, fired one up, and took a long drag. He sighed with the contentment of nicotine bliss. "Man, I needed that." He exhaled the smoke in a dragon's breath plume and said, "So what's up, sheriff?"

"How much do you know about Dale and Scooby?"

Raff shrugged. "I'd say I catch them both at least five or six times a year. Usually over in Saranac Lake or Tupper but they've definitely started to hit Whisper Falls, too."

"What can you tell me about them?"

"You mean aside from the fact that they're both junkie assholes and slaves to the meth?" Raff chuckled and took another drag from his cancer stick.

"Yeah, that part I already know."

"Well, I can tell you that Scooby is originally from Wisconsin and that his dad's a plumber."

"Not that far back. Just whatever info you have on them once they showed up in Whisper Falls."

"Gotcha." Raff pondered for a minute. "Well, Scooby used to be a painter. He worked for Henry Hutt, the real estate guy. You know him?"

Stone nodded.

"Scooby painted apartments, houses, for him. Then he got into the gack and now he can barely function."

"That's what that shit does to people," said Stone.

Raff nodded in agreement. "As for Dale, he rolled into town already junkie'd up. From what I've heard, he was causing trouble over in Rochester so the cops gave him a bus ticket here and told him to piss off and not come back or else."

Stone knew that happened to rural towns more than people realized. The urban areas viewed them as dumping grounds for their undesirables. Most of the forced transplants quickly hopped a bus to another city, but it looked like Dale had decided to stick around.

"One other thing," Raff said. "Not sure you're aware, but Scooby and Dale? They hate each other's guts."

"I didn't know that," Stone said.

"Yeah, they can't stand each other." Raff dropped his

cigarette stub and crushed it under his boot-heel, grinding it into the pavement. "Don't know all the details, but they got into a fight in Blue Line Sporting Goods about a month ago and I had to break them up. They were going at it like they *really* hated each other. Game on, fists a-flyin', no mercy."

"Guess both of them being meth addicts wasn't enough to give them a common bond," Stone said.

"Believe it or not, they used to live together. Shared a singlewide over in that trailer park just outside of town until Scooby threw Dale out. Lord knows roommates can drive each other crazy."

"So they were friends at one point at least."

"Whatever friendship they had is long gone," Raff said. "Nothing but hate now, but like I said, I don't know why. But from what I hear, they would both prefer the other in a body bag."

"Any chance it was a lover's quarrel?"

Raff shook his head. "I've seen them both with tweaker babes hanging off their arms. They're not gay."

Stone grinned. "Tweaker babes?"

Raff grinned back. "Yeah, tweaker babes. Don't act like you don't know what I'm talking about, sheriff."

"Sorry, not really my type."

"Yeah, I'm guessing you're more into the Holly Bennett type." Raff's grin widened.

"None of your damn business," Stone replied, but his light tone let Raff know that he wasn't really mad about the comment.

"Anyway," Raff said. "Scooby and Dale aren't the brightest crayons in the box. Whatever beef they've got going on is all kinds of toxic, from what I hear. The only thing they really care about is meth." He shrugged. "That's about all I can tell you."

"That's plenty," Stone said. "Appreciate the help."

"No problem."

Raff walked to his car, climbed in, and drove off into the night. Stone stayed outside for a while longer, Stetson tilted back as he stared up at the stars spackling the clear, velvet-black sky. His head was full of questions to which he had no answers.

FOURTEEN

THE NEXT MORNING dawned as crisp and clear as the night that preceded it, the brittle rays of the sun doing little to relieve the icy, invigorating edge in the air.

It was a good day for a drive and Stone decided he would check on Luisa's parents. Deputy Valentine had reported that they had both taken the news of their daughter's death badly, with Mrs. Valdez having to be sedated.

Stone completely understood.

When he lost his own daughter, he had plunged into oceans of absolute grief, utterly inconsolable. His wife Theresa had suffered the same fate, and instead of helping each other swim to the surface, they had both drowned alone and doomed their marriage in the process. Sometimes tragedy brings couples closer together; in their case, it tore them apart, and they divorced soon thereafter. Stone had thought their love could withstand anything, but a dead child turned out to be too much of a burden for that stricken love to bear.

Eventually his faith in God pulled him through, but he emerged on the other side of grief a broken man.

Putting himself back together had not been easy and in time he realized he would never really be "back together" again. A piece of his soul had died with Jasmine and that's just the way it would always be. Accepting it had been hard. Learning how to live with it had been even harder.

So yeah, he could sympathize with the Valdez's better than most.

He drove out to the cottage they were living in, thanks to the benevolence of Henry Hutt. He passed the Bennett house on the way and wondered if Lizzy had gone to school today or had stayed home to deal with her own grief over losing her friend. Holly would be at the diner, slinging plates of hash and eggs to hungry patrons.

He arrived at the Valdez residence a couple minutes later. The cottage was modest by local standards but done up in a quaint, cozy Adirondack style to give it some character. Hutt himself was in the driveway when Stone pulled in.

"Morning, Henry." Stone exited the Blazer and walked over to the landlord. "How's it going?"

"Fine, thanks. Just here to take care of a few repairs." He pointed at a toolbox in the open trunk of his car, then added, "Terrible news about Luisa." He lowered his voice even though there was nobody else around. "I know it's not very Christian of me, preacher, but I kind of hope whoever did that to her dies a horrible death."

"You're right, not very Christian," Stone agreed. "But understandable. How are her parents holding up?"

"Not good." Hutt shook his head sadly. "Mom's a mess, as you can imagine. But her dad, Alberto, is trying to stay strong for both of them. I guess all they can do is put one foot in front of the other at this point. Grief or not, the world keeps turning, you know?"

"I know it all too well," Stone replied.

"Anyway, if you're looking for them, they went back to work this morning. Alberto said they couldn't afford to just sit around and cry about Luisa."

"What exactly does Alberto do for work?"

Hutt frowned. "Now that you mention it, I'm not really sure. Want me to ask him when I see him?"

"I'll figure it out," Stone said.

He said farewell to Hutt and got back in the Blazer, heading east back toward Whisper Falls. The trees rose tight and high on either side of the road, revealing nothing more than a narrow strip of sky above. He glanced up and saw a bald eagle soar into view, carving a wide-winged silhouette across the ribbon of blue. He was admiring the raptor's grace when his cellphone rang. He put it on speaker.

"This is Stone."

"It's Dennis Fox. Got a second?"

"Sure." The eagle disappeared from view, probably heading over to one of the secluded ponds to hunt for fish. "What's up?"

"Got the chemical analysis reports from the burn sites."

"And?"

"Long story short, we found toluene, anhydrous ammonia, and pseudoephedrine at three of the four sites.

Stone understood the significance immediately. They were all common chemicals with individual uses, but the only reason to combine them was in the manufacturing of methamphetamine. They had suspected meth-cooking was involved in some of the fires, but now they had definitive proof.

"You said three of the four sites. Which one was clean?"

"The Gunther place. We didn't find any of that shit there. Just in the RV, shack, and storage unit."

"So the Gunther fire isn't connected to our meth problem."

"Doesn't look like it."

"Good to know. Thanks, chief."

"What's your next move?"

"Apply pressure and see if I can get something to crack."

———

Stone looked through the one-way mirror at the interview room where Dale slumped at the stainless-steel table, staring off into space with the blasted, red-rimmed gaze of a jonesing junkie.

The withdrawal effects were obvious. Dale twitched, grimaced, and shifted constantly in his seat like he had an infestation of fire ants in his boxers. Time to crank up the pressure.

Stone tightened down his Stetson and stepped into the interview room.

"Morning, Dale." Stone exaggerated his Texas accent as he flipped a chair around and sat on it backwards, resting his muscular arms along the back. "Sleep well?"

"Screw you, man. Go blow a cow or something."

Stone smiled thinly. He had been trained in interrogation tactics during his warrior days and knew that often the best approach was to form a bond with the subject, put them at ease, lend a "sympathetic" ear.

He had no intention of doing that here.

"Missing it?" he asked.

"Missing *what*?" Dale spat.

"Meth," Stone replied. "The only thing that can stop the hell that's burning up your veins right now."

Dale snorted. "Like you know anything about it."

"I know what can make it stop." Stone reached into

his shirt pocket and produced a small glassine baggie loaded with blue dust.

Dale's eyes snapped immediately to the baggie, watching intently, like a mangy tomcat being taunted by catnip. He looked utterly transfixed. His tongue poked out and slowly licked his dry, trembling lips.

Stone flicked the baggie, making the blue dust jump.

"They say this stuff is like heaven on earth. That right, Dale? Bet a snort of his would make you feel real damn good right about now."

Stone let the insinuated promise hang there. Desperation seized Dale's eyes and Stone could tell the junkie had swallowed the hook. It was dirty pool, no doubt, but Stone didn't care. Thinking about Luisa Valdez's burned corpse kept any misgivings at bay. He needed answers and he intended to get them, even if that meant using drugs as a carrot to an addict.

The hook was set. Time to reel in the fish, even if that meant tearing out his guts in the process.

"I could let you have some of this." Stone shook the baggie. "Kind of like an incentive program. Our little secret."

He dropped the baggie back in his pocket.

"All you've got to do is answer a few questions."

Dale was breathing heavy now. It almost sounded lustful. His eyelids drooped to half-mast. At first glance, it seemed like he had suddenly lost interest without the baggie in view.

But Stone knew better. Dale was gathering his strength, marshaling his inner resources, tapping into his bottomed-out reserves. The narcotic need rushing through his veins had pretty much shot his self-control to pieces. All he would be thinking about right now was the packet of powder in Stone's pocket.

To a junkie like Dale, it was the only thing that mattered.

"What do you want to know?" he asked dully.

Gotcha, Stone thought. Aloud he said, "When you shoplift, you like cold medicine."

It wasn't really a question but Dale swallowed hard and nodded anyway.

"Cold medicine," Stone repeated. "And things like cleaning fluid that contain ammonia. And petroleum products that contain toluene."

Still not a question but Dale nodded again. Sweat popped out on his forehead and he looked pale, like bones left lying in a graveyard.

"All those chemicals, they have something in common. Do you know what it is?"

Dale shook his head.

"They're all used to cook this." Stone patted the baggie in his pocket. "Kind of amazing that somebody can cook up heaven using everyday shit stolen from a convenience store."

"Just tell me what you want." Dale spoke loudly and aggressively. Not quite a yell, but close. Somehow his face turned even paler and took on a sickly gray cast, like the belly of a dead fish. His eyes flitted in their sockets.

"Fires are popping up all over town from somebody cooking meth," said Stone. "And now a young girl is dead, burned to death, and I'm betting the two are related. So what I want, Dale, is for you to tell me who's doing the cooking. Give me a name and then I'll give you what you want." He patted his pocket again.

Dale's jaw clenched, veins bulging in his neck as some kind of internal struggle took place. He clearly wanted his fix, probably felt like he needed it more than anything in the world. But there was something else going on, too, and Stone recognized it immediately.

Fear.

Dale was scared out of his mind. And it had nothing to do with the narcotic craving scorching his system. When he opened his mouth to speak, it wasn't to give Stone a name.

"I want a lawyer," Dale said emphatically. "I want a phone call, right now, and I want a lawyer."

Stone frowned. "You're making a mistake."

"I want a damn lawyer, you hear me? Gimme a goddamned phone! I wanna talk to Scott Slidell right fucking now!"

———

Just as he had with Scooby before him, Scott Slidell engaged in some slick-tongued legal wrangling and managed to get Dale released pending a court hearing.

Despite being a preacher, bound by the biblical commandment to love his neighbors, Stone had never liked Slidell. The attorney was a shallow, feckless man who camouflaged his naked avarice and willingness to bend every rule with a veneer of cheap charm and glamor. Fancy speech, tailored suits, flashy watches, styled haircuts...that was Scott Slidell. His utter disdain for law enforcement just completed the scummy package.

Stone tried not to hate the guy, but it was so damn hard.

"I suppose I should thank you." Slidell stood in the doorway of Stone's office, briefcase in hand. Somewhere outside, Dale was now walking free. Probably already on the prowl for his next dose of meth.

"Thank me for what?" Stone asked, a growl in his tone.

"You keep arresting these guys and they keep calling

me. It's a golden circle of symbiosis, wouldn't you agree?"

"I don't think you and I will ever agree on anything."

"Come now, sheriff. We're actually on the same side, are we not?"

"What side is that?"

"The side of the angels, of course." Slidell practically beamed, steadfast in his belief that his work was righteous. "You arrest suspects and then I swoop in and ensure their rights are protected. After all, society should not be expected to tolerate an abuse of authority by law enforcement..." He let the implied accusation hang there.

"I'm more worried about drug abuse than abuse of authority," Stone said. He picked up a pen designed to look like a .50 caliber cartridge and twirled it between his fingers, wishing Slidell would just go away.

"That's certainly understandable," Slidell replied. "Drug abuse is a plague, even up here in God's country. Your efforts to combat it are laudable, though I must confess that from where I'm standing, it looks like you're targeting little fish."

"I'm not targeting anyone. Just trying to get to the bottom of these fires and figure out who's behind our meth problem."

"Honestly, I think drugs are a matter of personal choice. Who are we to say what people should be allowed to put into their own bodies?" Slidell seemed to have forgotten that just moments ago he had agreed drug abuse was a plague. "We should just decriminalize all of them."

"Another thing you and I will never agree on," said Stone.

"Oh, come on, sheriff." Slidell's grin was greasy, his tone chiding. "It's just a little methamphetamine. Stop harassing the users and go after the dealers. You know, the big fish, the chemical chefs doing the cooking."

"That's what I'm trying to do."

"By any means necessary? My client informs me you offered him narcotics in exchange for information."

"I think your client misunderstood what I was saying."

"When I file a motion for a copy of the interview room's video footage, I wonder what it will reveal."

"Nothing." Stone shrugged. "I forgot to turn it on."

"How convenient." Slidell shook his head in mock sadness. "This will not end well for you, sheriff."

Stone smiled but the warmth never reached his eyes. "We're done here, counselor. You know where the door is."

FIFTEEN

THAT NIGHT, Stone decided it was time to track down Scooby, give his tree a hard shake, and see what rotten fruit fell out. Somebody knew something and Stone's patience was wearing thin.

He didn't tell any of his deputies where he was going. Nobody needed to know about this visit. He just climbed into the Blazer and headed for the trailer park on the outskirts of town where Scooby lived.

As he crossed the old railroad tracks, Stone forced himself to stay calm and not get frantic to solve this case. Or cases, plural, if you considered each fire and Luisa's murder as separate events. Frantic men made mistakes. The key here was to keep his mind cool, his emotions under control.

Easier said than done when he kept remembering what Luisa's charred corpse looked like.

He had taken the soft approach with Dale. Not his favorite style, but appropriate given the official setting. Regardless of what crime shows and movies depicted, the days of cops beating suspects to bloody pulps in the interview room was long gone.

But out here, away from the station, with no witnesses? Yeah, he could lean on Scooby hard. If the guy was home, he might be in for a rough ride.

He had the road to himself this time of night. He could feel little spikes of adrenaline pulsing in his system, little burbling of heat in his guts.

The route snaked along the river, taking him closer to his intended prey. A few minutes later, he saw the streetlight that illuminated the entrance to the trailer park. It glowed a sickly yellow. In the heat of summer, moths could be found flitting around the faintly-buzzing bulb, but it was too cold for that right now. Bug season was short-lived up here in the Adirondacks.

He parked the Blazer just inside the entrance. Rolling up to Scooby's door in the truck would alert the meth addict to the presence of law enforcement and give him a chance to bolt. Stone didn't want Scooby to know he was coming.

He walked toward the rundown single-wide on the far back lot. Some of the trailers he passed had porch lights on but the illumination didn't reach out here to the dirt lane that ran down the center of the park, so Stone walked in shadows. The brim of his Stetson threw his face into total darkness. In symbolic mimicry, the clouds overhead scuttled across the face of the moon and shrouded its silver glow.

Music thumped inside Scooby's trailer as Stone approached. It sounded like a whole rap concert happening in there. Stone couldn't believe the neighbors weren't screaming at the meth-head to turn it down. The windows were literally rattling in their frames from the hip-hop slap-down beats punching the air like sonic fists.

The music—if you could call it that—did nothing to improve Stone's mood. He hated rap. Because of his cowboy hat and old west attitude, most people automatically assumed he liked country, but he was really more of a rock 'n' roll kind of guy.

A silhouette passed in front of the window. Looked like Scooby—or at least someone—was home. Stone resisted the urge to just light a match, set the place ablaze, and see what kind of rats came scurrying out with their tails on fire.

The wind wasn't much, but it was cold, biting into his eyes and making him squint as he walked up the rickety metal steps to the main door. The thumping music inside drowned out any sounds he made, meaning whoever was in there was oblivious to his presence.

Stone reckoned it had to be warmer inside so he went ahead and kicked in the door.

Scooby stood in the kitchen area, caught off guard by Stone's violent entry. He wore a black hoodie, gray sweatpants, and sneakers without laces. He got over his shock in less than two seconds and dashed for the other door.

Stone was on him in two steps. He grabbed Scooby by the back of the neck and threw him against the wall. A framed photograph of the cast of *The Dukes of Hazzard* fell to the floor with a crash.

"Hey, man, what the hell? I didn't do anything!" Scooby twisted around, eyes wide and wild, desperate to get away.

Stone slammed a punch into his gut. He pulled the blow at the last second, his knuckles barely sinking in an inch. But the junkie howled as if his intestines had just flattened against his spinal column. Not that it mattered; the music was so loud, nobody could hear him scream.

"I see your mouth works," Stone rasped. "Good, because you and I are gonna have a little chat."

Scooby pushed off the wall. Stone grabbed him by the throat, threw him back, and squeezed. Scooby immediately went slack, realizing further resistance was pointless.

"There's nowhere to run," Stone said. "You done trying?"

"Yeah." The word came out choked. Scooby reached up and pulled on Stone's wrist, trying to free his throat. It was like trying to pry open a vise using a feather.

Stone kept up the pressure on Scooby's trachea for another few seconds, then let go. "You better be."

"What the hell you want, man? Why are you in my house?"

"I'm not here to read you your rights, you can bet on that." Stone pushed up the brim of his Stetson. "This is an unofficial visit."

"Yeah, I kind of figured that out when you kicked down my door, punched me in the stomach, and tried to choke me to death."

Stone's lips peeled back from his teeth in a mirthless smile. "If I wanted you dead, you would be."

"You sound like Chuck Norris."

"I'll take that as a compliment."

"It wasn't."

"You'll change your tune if I kick your teeth down your throat," Stone said. "And that's what I'm going to do if somebody doesn't start telling me who's cooking meth, setting fires, and burning little girls in my town."

"I didn't do any of that shit!"

"But I'm betting you know who did."

"Even if I did, I wouldn't tell you. I ain't no snitch."

"I'll take that as a yes."

"Take it up the ass, is what I heard about you," Scooby sneered.

"Taking it up the ass is what's going to happen to you when I stick murder one charges on you, throw you in prison, and let the convicts know that you killed a kid."

"Whoa! Slow your roll, man!" Scooby suddenly sounded worried. "That's some bullshit! Hell, I ain't even under arrest."

"You are now," said Stone. "Somebody has to take the fall for all the shit going on around here and you'll make a fine Judas goat."

"I ain't no goddamned goat!"

Stone grabbed Scooby's shoulder, spun him around, and slapped cuffs on his wrists.

"Hey!"

Stone started going through Scooby's pockets. "Got anything in here I need to know about? Needles, knives, guns?"

"No."

Stone pulled a capped syringe from Scooby's hoodie pocket. "Here's a needle." He dropped it on the counter. "And a knife." He took out a brand-new folding Buck knife with a rubber grip and dropped it beside the syringe.

"Damn, forgot all about those. Yeah, I got a needle. And a knife." Scooby sounded sheepish.

"Anything else?"

"A lighter, some cigarettes."

Stone took a crumpled pack of Marlboros from Scooby's pocket and added it to the collection on the counter. "Don't you know those cancer sticks will kill you?"

"I smoke meth. Pretty sure cigarettes aren't my biggest problem."

"Point taken."

"You done yet?"

"No."

"Oh, for the love of…"

Stone's hand came out of Scooby's pocket holding a key affixed to a ring with a red plastic tag on it. The tag had white lettering stamped on it that read:

CRESCENT STORAGE
Whisper Falls, NY

"Tell me about this," Stone said.

"Found it in a dumpster," Scooby replied.

"Sure you did." Stone spun Scooby around again and shoved him against the wall. "Know what I think? I think you're the one renting the storage unit that burned the other night. I think you camped out in there while you cooked meth."

For once, Scooby kept his mouth shut. Just stared off into space as if, by sheer force of will, he could make himself disappear.

Stone pinned him with icy eyes. "You won't be so quiet if I start putting bullets in your kneecaps."

"You're bluffing," Scooby snorted. "You won't do that. You're a cop and torturing people is against the law."

Stone leaned in close, his breath hot in the junkie's face. "I'll let you in on a little secret. I don't give a damn about the law when it comes to getting justice for that young girl. I'll shoot out your knees, shoot off your balls, then shoot you in the guts and watch you die if that's what it takes."

Scooby's eyes bugged out of his head. "What the hell kind of sheriff are you? Wait...ain't you a preacher, too? What the hell kind of *preacher* are you?"

"What can I say?" Stone growled. "I'm in an Old Testament kind of mood tonight. That happens when somebody burns a girl to death and dumps her body in the woods."

"Maybe the bitch committed suicide. That ever cross your mind?" Scooby smirked. "Maybe she wanted to go out in a *blaze* of glory."

The rage rose up swiftly, coursing through Stone's veins like rapids. He seized Scooby by his grimy wife-beater and slammed him against the wall, once, twice, three times. He wasn't gentle about it either. In fact, the third blow was so hard that for a moment he wondered if he had broken the junkie's back. He wouldn't have cared if he did.

"Think this is funny?" Stone rasped. "A girl is dead and I'm betting you had something to do with it."

"You ain't got nothing—"

Stone's fist crashed into Scooby's jaw like a sledge-hammer. The junkie's head whipped to the side as his defiant words got shut off mid-sentence.

Stone told himself to be careful. He was angry, worked up into a killing lather, enraged enough to tear somebody apart with his bare hands. Scooby made an easy, convenient target. But while he had his suspicions that the junkie was involved in—or at least had knowl-edge of—Luisa's death, what he didn't have was solid proof. He needed to resist the temptation to snap Scoo-by's neck.

For now.

He pulled Scooby off the wall and shoved him down in a recliner that had more cigarette burns than fabric. Stuffing bulged from rips in the flattened cushion like a ruptured sausage. "Don't move."

Stone stepped over the fallen picture and picked up a knapsack flung on the couch. It looked like the same one Scooby had been wearing the other night when Stone busted him for shoplifting. He peeled back the zipper and looked inside.

Scooby had been at it again. Just like the junkie couldn't stop smoking meth, he couldn't stop shoplifting either. Cans of beer and microwavable junk food formed the bulk of the load but there was cold medicine stuffed in there as well, along with some items from the sporting goods store.

Including a can of lighter fluid. Same brand as the one they'd taken off Dale.

Might mean something, might not. Like Dennis Fox had pointed out, lighter fluid was sold all over town. But it definitely upped his suspicion that Scooby knew something about the fires and Luisa's murder. Plenty of people bought lighter fluid. Not many of them walked around with it in their knapsacks.

He once again resisted the urge to put a bullet in Scooby.

Instead, he held up the can of lighter fluid. "Look at that. Same kind that was used to kill Luisa Valdez." Of course, he didn't actually know that, but neither did Scooby. Stone watched carefully for the junkie's reaction, some subtle giveaway of guilt.

Scooby blanched a bit but didn't say a word. Just stared straight ahead, stone-faced. He didn't even ask for a lawyer when Stone dragged him outside, threw him in the back of the Blazer, and hauled him off to jail.

SIXTEEN

THE NEXT MORNING, Deputy Valentine finally made contact with the owner of Crescent Self Storage Facility who confirmed that Martin 'Scooby' Taylor was the renter of the burned-out unit.

"He's really pissed about the fire," Valentine said to Stone as they both stared through the one-way mirror into the interview room. Scooby sat alone at the table, looking calm one second, all fidgety the next. "Says he's going to sue Scooby."

"Just imagine the financial windfall he'll reap," Stone said sarcastically. "He'll be able to afford Raman noodles for at least a week."

Valentine laughed and headed back to his desk.

Stone squared his shoulders and walked into the interview room. Time to buckle down to business. He still kind of wished he had just beaten a confession out of Scooby in his trailer last night.

"Morning." Just as he had done with Dale yesterday, Stone reversed the chair, straddled it, and folded his arms across the back. "Had your breakfast yet?"

"No!" Scooby shook his head, his red curls flailing

around like Medusa's snakes. "Your dumbass deputy didn't feed me."

"That's a shame. A growing boy needs to eat."

"I'm a man, not a boy."

"A man we've arrested seventeen times in the past year. That may be some kind of record."

"More like police brutality, is what it is."

"You want to know what's brutal? The amount of merchandise you've stolen from stores in this town. Over ten thousand dollars."

"Ask me if I give a shit."

Stone wanted to bounce the junkie's face off the table until his nose looked like a splattered strawberry. He resisted the urge but it took some willpower.

Instead of violently rearranging Scooby's facial features, Stone asked him, "Do you know what you steal more than anything else?"

"This is stupid…"

"Cold medicine," Stone said. "That's your most common item. In the past twelve months, you've boosted over two hundred boxes of the stuff. You got a bad cough or something?"

"I steal all kinds of stuff," Scooby snapped. "Mostly just what I need to survive. In case you ain't noticed, I'm fucking poor."

"Not too poor to afford a storage unit."

"It's not mine."

"Cut the crap, Scooby. The owner confirmed it's yours."

"Okay, so it's mine. So what?"

"So what were you using it for?"

"Nothing."

"Really? You waste money on a storage unit—money you could use for drugs and food—and do nothing with it?"

Scooby shifted in his chair. "What the hell do you think I do with it? I use it to store stuff."

"Like chemicals?"

Scooby grew very still.

"Yeah, chemicals," Stone repeated. "Like ammonia, toluene, rubbing alcohol."

Scooby smirked. "That's not the kind of alcohol I drink. Sorry."

"But it is the kind you like to steal. Almost two hundred bottles this year alone."

Scooby stopped smirking but said nothing.

"You want to know what I think?"

"No."

Stone ignored him. "I think I was wrong about you. You're not too stupid to cook meth. In fact, I think you were using the storage unit to cook up the base."

"You charging me?"

"Hell, yeah, I'm charging you. Unless you tell me something that changes my mind. I'll hold you on the drug charges while I get the evidence to prove you killed Luisa Valdez."

"I didn't kill that girl!" Scooby said, almost yelling. Then he slumped back in his chair, heaved a sigh of resignation, and said, "It was Dale."

"Dale killed Luisa?"

"No." Scooby shook his head. "At least, I don't think so. Hell, I don't know. But that's not what I meant. I meant it was Dale using the storage unit. He asked if he could use it months ago. I haven't even been there since last summer. Whatever happened in there, you'll have to ask Dale about."

"I will." Stone narrowed his eyes. "And I'm still going to figure out who burned that girl alive."

"Good for you, sheriff." Scooby smiled, exposing his

black, rotting teeth. "Now get me my goddamned lawyer."

———

Later that afternoon, Stone got a call from Captain Chandler of the RCMP. They exchanged pleasantries and then Chandler said, "Things are heating up here with our nightclub shooting."

"Heating up how?"

"We've been working in tandem with the CBSA." He paused. "That's Canada Border Services Agency for you foreigners."

"Smartass." Stone smiled. "I know what it is."

"Anyway, we managed to get some wiretaps authorized and long story short, we think our suspects are involved in some cross-border action. We've identified multiple vehicles that we think belong to some of the major players. I'll send you the list in case they show up in your neck of the woods."

"Wouldn't you flag the vehicle and have them stopped at the border?"

"We don't have enough on them yet to stop them from crossing. The lawyers would eat us alive." Chandler mumbled something that wasn't very clear but sounded like a four-syllable profanity. "I hate lawyers."

"Shoot the list over to me," Stone said. "If any of the vehicles show up around here, I can keep an eye on them, see what they're up to."

"Thanks, Stone. I'd really like to nail these bastards. They shot up Toronto, for god's sake! It's supposed to be one of the safest cities in Canada."

Stone wasn't sure there was anywhere truly safe anymore. Even his patch of God's country up here in the Adirondacks was seeing its fair share of drugs and violence. Granted, it wasn't an epidemic of crime like you experienced in the major metropolitan areas, but it still meant the darkness was pushing against the light, evil creeping in where it had once been unwelcome.

Things change, he thought. And often not for the better. Sometimes the old ways are the best ways.

He exchanged farewells with Chandler, promising to keep in touch. As he put down the phone, he found himself thinking about criminal enterprises, meth cooks, murdered children. And he found himself hating the world just a little more than usual.

SEVENTEEN

"ANY EVIDENCE LINKING Scooby or Dale—or both —to Luisa Valdez's murder is circumstantial." Stone sat across the table from Dennis Fox, hands wrapped around a cup of coffee. It was almost peak dinner time and the Birch Bark Diner was starting to fill up. The evening darkness outside pressed up against the windows. "They've both retained Scott Slidell to represent them so I doubt we're going to get a confession."

"Same with the fires," Fox said. "There's just nothing concrete to pin on either one of them. Walking around with lighter fluid doesn't prove a damn thing."

"Not much we can do without proof."

"Hell of a thing, watching the guilty skate free."

"Maybe karma will deal its own justice."

"Any chance those two clowns are working together?"

"Unlikely," Stone said. "They hate each other. Can't imagine them throwing down together on a drug deal, let alone a murder. Hell, Scooby even tried to snitch out Dale for the fire in his storage unit."

"So we're pretty much nowhere," Fox said in frustration.

"It'll work itself out." Stone sounded more confident than he actually felt.

Fox nodded but didn't say anything, glancing outside as if the cold autumn night held the answers he sought. Holly drifted over to their table, smiling at Stone in that way that always made him feel warm inside. She had invited him over for dinner tonight.

"Need more coffee?" she asked. She looked pointedly at the clock; it was 6:00 p.m. Her shift was done.

"Coffee time is over," Stone said, catching her look. "Time for something stronger."

"I've got a meeting up in Milford." Fox dropped some money on the table. "Some kind of firefighting equipment demonstration. I'm only going 'cause there's free beer."

"There's beer here."

"Yeah, but it's not free."

"Point taken," said Stone.

"See you around, sheriff."

Stone and Holly watched as Fox left the diner and crossed the parking lot to his truck. His taillights glowed red in the darkness as he drove away.

Stone turned to Holly. "How's Lizzy doing?"

She slid into the seat Fox had just vacated. "Not good," she sighed. "Spends all her time holed up in her room. She's only been to school once since Luisa was killed and she came home after lunch, couldn't even make it all the way through the day. She and Luisa had become good friends, so this hit her pretty hard."

Stone felt anger surge inside him. He longed for a focus for his rage, someone to visit justice upon for Luisa's murder. It bothered him that he could kill so easily when the target deserved it, but not enough to stay his hand.

"I was hoping maybe you could talk to her." Holly's eyes were pleading. "She trusts you, Luke. Maybe she'll open up to you in a way she can't with me."

"I'll try." He gave her a soft, reassuring smile.

She reached across the table and squeezed his arm. "You're a good guy, sheriff. Or preacher. Or whatever the hell you are right now."

"Right now I'm just a guy talking to a girl."

"You ever do more than talk?" she asked mischievously.

"Sure," he replied. "When the time is right."

"Any idea when that will be?"

"I'll let you know."

"When?"

He gave her a crooked grin. "When the time is right."

She laughed and stood up. "C'mon, let's get you that drink. I'm ready for one myself."

Stone followed her out of the diner. They crossed the parking lot to their vehicles, breath fogging in the cold. An icy mist dampened the air, the threat of winter snapping at the town. Before long, the hard, frozen ground would be covered with snow. Hell, based on the ice crystals hanging in the night air, the snow might very well arrive by morning.

At Holly's place, she opened the front door, dropped her purse on the table, and called out, "Lizzy?"

No answer. "Probably up in her room," Holly said.

Stone closed the door behind him, shrugged out of his coat, and took off his Stetson. "I can go talk to her."

Holly looked at him gratefully. "I think that might do some good, honestly. I'll fix us some drinks and get dinner going in the meantime."

Stone went upstairs. The door to Lizzy's room was closed, muffled music leaking out into the hall. Stone didn't recognize the band, some kind of rap infused with Mexican beats.

He knocked on the door. "Lizzy? It's Luke."

The song cut out and the door opened. Lizzy peeked out, wearing a pair of baggy sweatpants and a mock-vintage Stryper t-shirt from their *To Hell With the Devil* tour. Stone smiled to himself. Now *that* was more his style of music.

"Hi, Luke." She mustered up a smile for him, though he could see it was tinged with sadness.

"Hey." Stone cocked his head, studying her. "You doing okay?"

"Yeah. Well, no." She swung the door open all the way. "Come on in."

Stone walked into her room. Posters decorated the wall, typical for any teenager. But unlike most teenagers —at least the ones Stone had encountered—the room was fairly neat and organized. No piles of dirty clothes heaped everywhere, no belongings flung haphazardly around, no kicked-off sneakers lying on the floor waiting to be tripped over.

Stone sat down at her desk, swinging the chair around so it faced her bed where she now sat, legs folded Indian-style, her laptop beside her. "What was that song you were listening to?" he asked.

"That's Bella. She's a Mexican rapper that Luisa got me hooked on." Lizzy picked up the laptop. "That song is called 'Life Lessons.' It was one of Luisa's favorites."

"Play it for me."

"You sure?" Lizzy smirked. "Figured Blake Shelton would be more your style."

"I'm actually more of a rock 'n' roll guy, but I'd still like to hear the song."

"Don't say I didn't warn you." Lizzy tapped a key on her laptop and the music started up, sinuous and funky.

Stone didn't care much for rap but he had to admit the singer had a cool voice and she put her tough, street-wise lyrics together really well. Lizzy's mood seemed to lighten as they listened to the song, the wisp of a smile crossing her face as she remembered her friend.

When the song finished, Lizzy talked, her voice soft and quiet. Stone just sat and listened, knowing that sometimes that was all a person needed. He felt Lizzy's connection with Luisa and found it remarkable that two girls from such different backgrounds, different countries, could share such a strong bond.

He lost track of time until Holly appeared in the doorway. "Dinner's ready, if you two are hungry." She looked at Lizzy. "I made cabbage rolls."

Lizzy visibly brightened. "My favorite," she said. "I'll be down in a couple minutes."

Stone joined Holly in the kitchen for a drink while they waited for Lizzy to come downstairs. He leaned a hip against the counter and sipped his Jack and Coke, lots of ice, easy on the Jack. Looking at Holly, he silently wondered where things would lead with her.

The look she was giving him made him realize that she was wondering the same thing. But she didn't say anything about it. Instead, she said, "You're really good with her. Thank you."

"She's a good kid. Makes me wonder what my daughter would have been like if she had lived to be a teenager."

"I'll bet she was an angel." Holly's eyes softened.

"No doubt about it." Stone took another drink, trying to wash down the lump in his throat. All these years later, it was still so damn hard to talk about Jasmine.

When Lizzy showed up, they sat down at the dining room table. Holly spooned out cabbage rolls from a dish as Lizzy talked about the Valdez family.

"They're really hard workers," she said. "Mr. Hutt gave Luisa's dad some handyman work when they first got here and said he worked harder than any man he'd ever met."

"Any idea what the dad is doing for work now?" Stone asked.

"He got a new job not too long ago," she replied. "Luisa was telling me about it. He was a driver or something, but she wasn't sure who he worked for."

"Like a cab driver or something?"

"I don't know." Lizzy shrugged. "I remember Luisa's mom wasn't happy about it, whatever it was. But Mr. Valdez insisted. Said it was good money and they needed it. He would do anything for his family. Very protective, too."

"Nothing wrong with that," Stone said.

"Oh, man, we were at Sloane's one day." Lizzy paused with a forkful of cabbage roll halfway to her mouth. "Mr. Valdez almost got into a fight with some guy."

Stone and Holly glanced at each other. Luisa's father seemed like a quiet man who kept his head down and avoided trouble. Certainly not the type to get involved in an altercation. Then again, Stone thought, what do we really know about him?

"What kind of fight?" Stone asked.

"I was hanging out with Luisa and her parents wanted to buy us ice cream. On the way, we stopped at Sloane's so they could pick up a few things they needed. When we came out of the store, that guy...I don't know his name, but he catches shoplifters?"

"Rafferty. We call him Raff," Stone said. "Loss prevention officer. Works Sloane's all the time."

"Yeah, him." Lizzy set down her fork, food forgotten as she told the story. "He was talking to some guy outside. Looked like a creep. Not an argument or anything, they were just talking. When we came out of the store, the creepy guy turned and saw Mr. Valdez and swore at him. Told him he was a loser for screwing up."

Stone asked, "What did the guy look like?"

"Bloodshot eyes. Really bad teeth. Red hair."

"Sounds like Scooby," Stone said. "He's one of our local meth-heads."

"Well, he and Mr. Valdez seemed to know each other," Lizzy said. "After the creepy Scooby guy called him a loser, Mr. Valdez tried to smooth things over. But Scooby started yelling, saying Mr. Valdez had messed up his chances and was going to pay for it."

Stone's face remained impassive but his mental gears were working overtime to process this new information.

"Mr. Valdez tried to stay cool but Scooby just kept at him. Called the whole family nasty names and said he was going to make sure they got sent back to where they came from. That's when Mr. Valdez blew up. Got right in Scooby's face and started cursing in Spanish."

"How do you know Spanish curse words?" Holly asked.

Lizzy shrugged, the corner of her mouth quirking up in a little smile. "Luisa taught me."

"So what happened next?" Stone asked.

"It looked like they were gonna fight, but they never actually threw punches. Mr. Valdez just kept clenching and unclenching his fists. He was really angry and you could tell he really wanted to hit Scooby, but he didn't."

Lizzy chose that moment to shovel the forkful of cabbage roll that she had momentarily forgotten into her mouth. Stone and Holly waited patiently as she chewed, swallowed, took a drink, and then finished the story.

"Anyway, the Scooby dude ended up spitting on the ground and walking away, still dropping f-bombs like he was going for some kind of world record. Mr. Valdez watched him leave then told Luisa and Mrs. Valdez to stay away from the guy. When Mrs. Valdez asked him how he knew Scooby, Mr. Valdez just shook his head and didn't say anything."

Stone absorbed this new information, adding it to the intel he already possessed. He didn't have all the pieces yet, but the puzzle was starting to take shape in his mind.

———

After dinner, Stone helped Holly with the dishes. Lizzy shrugged into her coat and boots.

"I'm going for a walk," she announced.

"It's dark out," Holly said.

"I'm sixteen, mom. Not exactly scared of the dark anymore. I just need to get out of my room, clear my head."

"Fine, but don't be long. You've got school tomorrow," Holly said. "And take a flashlight so cars can see you."

"What cars?" Lizzy muttered. "We live out in the middle of nowhere." But she grabbed a flashlight off the shelf by the door before she headed out into the night.

"She gonna be all right?" Stone asked.

"She's fine," Holly replied. "She does this all the time. One of the advantages of living out in the country, away from town. You can just take a stroll down the road whenever the mood strikes you."

"I was talking about Luisa," Stone clarified. "Losing a friend is a hard blow. Think Lizzy will be all right?"

"She's a tough kid. Will she be all right?" Holly shrugged. "I think so. I *hope* so."

"Me, too," Stone replied, and said a silent prayer.

———

Lost in her own thoughts, Lizzy wandered down the road.

A thin fog blanketed the area, warmth from the ground seeping into the cold autumn air to generate ghostly tendrils that snaked around her ankles. The mist oozed through the shadowed forest on either side of the road, suffused with the silvery light of the moon glowing in the star-spackled sky above.

Lizzy found herself amused by the way the low-lying fog coalesced and eddied around her as she walked, like she was passing through a series of weightless gauze curtains. The effect was almost hypnotizing. Or maybe she was just looking for something, anything, to take her mind off the pain.

The loss of Luisa stung, vibrating in her chest like a stuck arrow. She doubted the hurt would ever go away. It felt like there was a giant hole in her heart.

Maybe she should just get used to it. Maybe her life was just meant to be hard, like she was cursed or something. Abused by her father, running away in the middle of the night, jerked all over the country by the WITSEC program, the attack by the survivalists earlier this year, now Luisa's death…it was easy to think that maybe God just hated her. She knew Stone wouldn't like her thinking that way, but she couldn't help it.

Headlights occasionally flashed by, punching holes in the fog and momentarily pulling her out of her gloomy thoughts. This wasn't a main road, but locals used it as a backcountry shortcut between Whisper Falls and Tupper Lake.

She had no way of knowing that one of the cars that went by, slowed down, and then sped back up, wasn't a local. She also had no way of knowing they were talking about her. If she could have heard what they were saying, she would have run for her life.

———

The black sedan contained three sets of eyes that all glanced at Lizzy as they drove past, sizing her up like predators hunting prey.

"That's her," the man in the backseat said. "She was tight with that Mexican bitch we burned. I saw her with the whole family one time at Sloane's."

"She was a friend of the girl?"

"Yeah, and her mom has the hots for the sheriff."

"Is that so?" The voice was female, smooth, and icy. "Perhaps another message is in order."

"You want me to turn around?" the driver asked.

"We pull over on this road at this time of night and try to grab her, she'll just run into the woods and we'll never find her."

"I could always ram her, break her legs. Then the bitch won't be able to go anywhere."

"Always ready to resort to violence, aren't you?"

"It's what you pay me for. And it's kind of my thing."

"A time and a place for everything and now is not the time or the place."

"What do you want to do?"

The woman turned her head and watched the trees rush past in the darkness. "We'll take her tomorrow morning."

EIGHTEEN

STONE WOKE up the next morning at 5:00 a.m. He immediately sat up in bed, a thought going through his mind.

Of course. Why didn't I see it before?

He threw back the covers, eliciting a grumbling groan from Max, who enjoyed nothing more than sleeping at the foot of the bed. The groan seemed to say, *Hey, man, it's too early for this nonsense.* Stone ignored the dog's protests, picked up his phone, and dialed the station.

"Garrison County Sheriff's Department." The Cajun drawl was unmistakably Catfish. "How can I help you?"

"It's Stone." He headed into the kitchen to make coffee. Max, begrudgingly awake, shambled behind to examine his food dish. "Sanchez or Valentine there yet?"

"Little early, boss. Even for Sanchez."

"Okay. As soon as they get in, this is what I want you to do."

Stone relayed his instructions quickly and carefully. Catfish had spent a lot of years in the military so he knew how to pay attention when orders were given. After Stone finished, the deputy relayed back the instructions, waited to receive confirmation, then promised he would make it happen. Stone thanked him and hung up.

He fed Max and then took a long, hot shower, planning his next moves. His plan held some risk but he needed to shake things up and see if he could rattle some pieces into place. It was going to be an interesting morning.

Stone toweled off, dressed, and poured that all-important first cup of coffee. Pulling on his jacket, he stepped out onto the front porch, Max on his heels, and sat down on the wooden Adirondack chair.

The large, wooded parsonage property was quiet this early in the morning. The crows had not yet begun to caw and the wild turkeys had not yet begun to gobble. Off to his right, just past the Crimson King maple tree he had planted last spring, a whitetail deer yearling emerged from the brush and browsed along the edge of the lawn.

Stone's life had not been easy but mornings like this made it easier to count his blessings.

He watched the sun come up over the mountains, sipping his coffee, content to steal a few moments of peace before the chaos of the day started. Max finished his morning patrol of the property and flopped down beside him.

Stone stroked the dog's scarred head and breathed deeply of the fresh, invigorating air, letting the cold and the caffeine fully wake him up. He felt the sand slipping through his internal hourglass and knew his moments of calm were coming to an end. He mentally rehearsed his plan one more time.

"Kind of a long shot, Max," he said. "We'll see if it pays off."

Max yawned, exposing large teeth that had served him well during his dogfighting days before Stone rescued him, and gave him a look that seemed to say, *Just as long as you make it home in time to give me my biscuit.*

Stone sat in the chilly silence until it was time to head to town. It was a beautiful late autumn morning but he couldn't help thinking that it all felt so fragile, like dead leaves waiting to be crushed by forces not yet known.

———

"Catfish, what are you still doing here?" Stone entered the sheriff's station and shrugged off his coat. "Your shift ended an hour ago."

"Just covering the desk while Valentine and Sanchez fetch those two yahoos you asked for." The tall, bearded Louisiana boy stretched in his chair. "Sanchez is en route with her package and Cade already wrangled his in."

"Good." Stone checked his watch. "Go home and get some sleep."

"I'll sleep when I'm dead, boss."

"Then go home and do whatever crazy Cajuns do on their downtime."

Catfish grinned. "You don't even wanna know."

"You're right, I don't."

Stone went into his office and caught up on some emails while he waited for Sanchez to arrive. About twenty minutes later, she stuck her head through the door.

"We're ready, sheriff."

Stone stood up and headed for the interview room. "Give me thirty seconds and then bring him in."

"Copy that, sir."

Stone walked into the interview room and found Dale sitting there, picking at the scabs on his arms. He looked up and sneered when he saw Stone.

"What the hell is this crap, man? You can't just drag me in here for no reason."

"Believe me," Stone said, "I've got a reason."

The door opened again. Dale looked up and his face melted with horror, quickly followed by hatred, as Sanchez shoved Scooby into the room.

"What the hell…?"

"I'm not sitting in here with him!" Scooby yelled.

"Sit down!" Stone's voice boomed like artillery in the confined space. Both meth-heads immediately quieted. Scooby dropped into a chair with a sullen expression on his face.

"I'll be right outside," Sanchez said, and exited the room.

Stone leaned against the wall and crossed his arms. "Neither one of you is being charged with anything at this point. Play straight with me, answer my questions, and you'll both be out of here in ten minutes."

This seemed to calm them down even further. They glanced at each other, then looked away. Scooby found a spot on the floor and stared at it intently. Dale just shrugged.

Stone said, "Dale, you reported the car that was found abandoned out in the woods."

"Yeah, so?" Dale seemed surprised to be asked about it. "The car was just sitting there, so I reported it."

"Not too far from where that RV burned, right?" Stone didn't wait for an answer, just turned his gaze to Scooby. "And you were renting the storage unit that burned."

Scooby firmed his lips, looked defiant for a moment, then relented and gave a short nod.

"You guys used to be friends."

Neither one of them said anything.

"In fact, you two used to live together. No doubt

scored drugs and got high together. Question is, what changed?"

They both stared at him. He had their full attention now.

"All these fires got me thinking," Stone said. "I've got two meth-heads tied to fires in places where it looks like meth was being cooked. Then this morning it hit me. The thing that could cause friction and end a friendship. Know what that is?"

Silence.

"Competition."

Both men fidgeted in their seats, as if the chairs had suddenly become uncomfortable. Stone smiled thinly. Looked like his hunch had been right.

"I think you're both cooking meth and setting fires, trying to burn each other out so you can control the production around here." Stone unfolded his arms and pushed away from the wall. "And I want to make it clear that if I find any more evidence to that effect, you'll both be facing murder charges. Welcome to the big league, boys."

"Murder?" Scooby gulped and looked worried.

"Hey," Dale croaked. "What's this murder crap?"

"Luisa Valdez. The girl burned to death out in the woods. You two are the primary suspects unless you can prove you didn't do it and tell me who did. Or keep your mouths shut and find yourselves looking at a death sentence." Stone opened the door. "Your call."

As both men stood up to leave, Dale muttered, "New York doesn't have the death penalty."

Stone gave him a cold, steely stare. "Who said anything about the state of New York?"

Dale swallowed hard and he and Scooby left, momentarily forgetting that they were mortal enemies now.

Deputy Sanchez waited until they were gone, then came over and asked, "Think they'll break?"

"If one of them killed the Valdez girl and the other one knows it, I think the one who didn't do it will break weak and give the other guy up to save his own ass," Stone said.

"Or they did it together and now they'll just dig in deeper."

"Possible." Stone shrugged. "We'll just have to wait and see."

———

The low-lying fog from the night before was still there as Lizzy waited at the end of her driveway for the school bus to pick her up. It lay thick on the ground, making her feel like she was standing in gray soup. Her feet felt cold in her sneakers and she debated running inside and changing into a pair of boots.

Before she could decide, a car pulled up in front of her.

Its headlights were on, slashing through the ground mist. The dark-tinted windows prevented her from seeing who was inside the black sedan, but she felt eyes fixed on her behind the smoked-out glass. The feeling of being watched when she couldn't see the watcher made her uneasy.

Lizzy stayed alert as the black car stopped, tires crunching on the gravel at the end of the driveway. She wasn't scared, just wary. This was a back-country road with nobody around to hear her scream if this turned out to be something more menacing than a lost driver asking for directions. A little caution wasn't out of place.

The passenger window purred down on its electric motor and a pretty blonde woman poked her head out.

"Sweetheart, you look cold standing out here." The accented voice sounded genuinely concerned. "Are you all right?"

Lizzy shrugged. "Just waiting for the bus." She looked past the woman and into the car. A slender man sat behind the wheel, his face wreathed in five o'clock shadow. Someone else sat behind him but she couldn't get a good look. "You lost?" Lizzy asked.

The woman smiled. "No, we know our way around these parts. We just saw you standing out here and thought we would check on you."

"I'm good," Lizzy said. "So unless there's something else…"

"Can we give you a ride to school? We're heading into town anyway."

Lizzy shook her head. "Thanks, but getting into a car with strangers? Not gonna happen." She smiled to take the edge off the words and make it clear no offense was intended. She wanted the car to just leave. She glanced down the road, hoping to see the bus coming.

"Smart girl. You're Holly's daughter, right?" The woman's smile broadened. "I know your mom. Works at the Birch Bark. Nice lady."

"Everyone in town knows my mom."

"It's just a ride."

"I'm not getting in the car with you."

"You sure about that?" the woman asked.

Lizzy felt a shiver run down her spine that had nothing to do with the cold. Something was wrong. Behind the friendly smile and helpful words, Lizzy sensed the woman was not a nice person. Call it teenage intuition.

"It's not safe out here," the woman said. "I can't in good conscience just leave you. Pretty sure a girl your age got burned alive out this way not too long ago."

Lizzy's eyes narrowed. "What did you just say?"

"You heard me. Now get in the car."

"Fuck you, lady."

"No, thanks, you're a little young for my tastes. But if you don't get in the car in the next ten seconds, my man Darius here will drive to the diner and shoot your mother in the head."

Lizzy's blood froze. "I'm friends with the sheriff," she said, the words just blurting from her mouth.

"Even better," the woman said. "Darius will kill him, too." A gun appeared in the woman's hand. "Do you need me to count down for you or can you do it in your head? You've got ten seconds."

"No need to count. I'll come with you." Lizzy's heart hammered in her chest. "Just leave my mom alone."

"Get in the back with Scooby," Yvonne said, and smiled wolfishly.

NINETEEN

STONE SHUFFLED papers in his office and waited for a call from Scott Slidell that never came. Apparently neither Dale nor Scooby had run sobbing to their lawyer to tell him that Stone had dragged them in for questioning. They were both probably hunkered down in some hovel trying to get high so they could forget they were prime suspects in a gruesome murder case.

Stone wondered how much longer he could resist the urge to just drag them both out into the woods and pump bullets into non-fatal parts of their anatomies until they fessed up. Neither one of them looked like they would be able to withstand much pain before breaking.

Easy to be defiant with a defense attorney standing by your side. Not so easy when you're all alone with a bullet in your kneecap.

His cellphone buzzed, pulling him away from thoughts of painful interrogation techniques. He looked at the screen and saw that it was Holly calling. He answered with a smile. "Hey."

Her words wiped the smile off his face.

"Luke, Lizzy is missing! She never made it to school

and she's not at home and she's not answering her phone!"

"Where are you?"

"I'm at the high school."

"I'll be right there."

———

Alana Prentiss, the principal, was waiting nervously in front of the high school when Stone pulled up and parked in the bus circle. She had a walkie-talkie in her hand and started talking the second Stone stepped out of the Blazer.

"I've got staff combing the building and grounds right now, sheriff," she said. A tall, serious black woman with a rich southern accent that always reminded Stone of his home state of Texas, Prentiss was all business. Wearing a pantsuit and coke-bottle glasses, she resembled a cross between Venus Williams and Henry Kissinger. "If she's on campus, we *will* find her, believe me."

"I have no doubt," said Stone, but his gut told him that Lizzy's disappearance had to do with something more nefarious than a kid skipping class. But he kept that thought to himself.

A scratchy voice came through the speaker of the walkie-talkie. "Ma'am, we finished a sweep of the sports fields and woods out back. No sign of her."

"Thank you." Prentiss lowered the radio and shook her head. "That's everywhere, sheriff. We checked all the classrooms, locker rooms, bathrooms, even the storage sheds, before you got here."

"Where's Holly?"

"Waiting for you in my office."

Stone followed the principal down a large, tiled corridor to the administration hub. Holly sat tensely in a chair in Prentiss' office, clutching her cellphone, staring at the screen as if begging it to ring and let her know her daughter was safe.

She surged to her feet when Stone walked in, throwing herself into his arms without hesitation. "Luke, she's gone!"

He held her tight and told her it would be okay, even though he knew that might be a lie. What was *not* a lie was that he would move heaven and earth to find Lizzy.

"She hasn't been missing long," he said, "so the odds are still in our favor.

She looked up at him, eyes wet with tears. "Do you think she's..." Her voice trailed off, unable to bring herself to say the word.

Dead.

"Don't even think it," Stone said firmly. *But if she is,* he silently told himself, *I swear to God I'll kill anyone who had a hand in it.*

TWENTY

RIDING in the shotgun seat of the Chevy Blazer, Holly said, "This is nothing like her, Luke."

"I know." What remained unspoken between them was the circumstances of Holly and Lizzy's arrival in Whisper Falls.

Holly's parting of ways with Lizzy's father had not been a normal, routine divorce. Jack 'Lucky Draw' Dawson had turned out to be a west coast mob boss with deep roots in organized crime. After he turned abusive, Holly had testified against him and helped put him behind bars. She and Lizzy were placed in the Federal Witness Protection Program, which is how they ended up in a small mountain town in upstate New York.

"Where's Jack?" Stone asked. "Any chance he's got something to do with this?"

"He's still rotting in Lompoc Federal Penitentiary, right where the judge put him." Holly's voice was grim. "So it's not my ex."

"Had to ask."

"I know."

Stone had already issued a BOLO. Anyone who wore

a badge in the tri-county area—cop, deputy, trooper—had their eyes peeled.

"We should check her computer," he said. "Emails, social media, that sort of thing. See if there's any clue there."

"I can probably access her accounts," Holly said. "She's pretty lax about that stuff."

"Give it a shot." Stone reached for the mike on his police radio. "I'm gonna have the Valdezes brought to the station."

"You don't think they had something to do with it, do you?"

"All I know is that someone killed their daughter and now her best friend is missing, too. So the last two girls to disappear around here were both connected to the Valdezes. Seems like a good place to start."

Holly nodded tightly. She trusted him.

Stone made the call, dispatching deputies to pick up Mr. and Mrs. Valdez. He prayed to God they didn't have anything to do with Lizzy's vanishing. Because if they did, *they* would be the ones praying to God.

To save them from Stone.

———

As they drove back to the station, Stone reflected how even the most rural, friendly, picturesque towns had a dark underbelly. Most of them hid it well, but it was still there, lurking, and Whisper Falls was no exception. The crime and corruption that had long ago claimed the big cities had slowly crept into small-town America. You could fight it—and Stone did—but it still just kept on coming.

As they entered the station, Deputy Drummond was behind the front desk. He greeted Stone and Holly with a cheery good morning that none of them actually felt, then said, "The Valdezes are in your office. Didn't want to make them wait in an interrogation room like a couple of suspects."

"Good call," Stone said.

"Not my first rodeo."

Holly was staring at her cellphone. "Still no answer to my texts." Panic quivered in her voice. Who could blame her? Her daughter was missing and her phone had gone dark. She was living a parent's worst nightmare.

Stone put a comforting hand on her shoulder. "We'll find her," he said. "That's a promise." He just hoped it was a promise he could keep.

They went into his office where the Valdezes waited. Alberto grasped Stone's hand and gave it a firm shake. A weary sadness etched his face. His wife, a nervous, slender woman, mustered up a smile and a little nod. It was the best she could do and Stone didn't blame her; she was still deeply grieving the loss of Luisa.

"Lizzy has gone missing," Stone said without preamble. "She never made it to school this morning. Any chance you've seen her?"

"No, *senor*," Alberto replied. He glanced at his wife, who shook her head. "We have not seen her. This is terrible news. Lizzy is a sweet girl, a good friend to our Luisa. May God rest her soul."

Stone wasn't sure if they wanted God to rest Luisa's soul or Lizzy's and he wasn't about to ask.

Mrs. Valdez said something in Spanish. Alberto listened and then translated. Stone didn't bother to tell them that he spoke Spanish. During his warrior days, he had lost count of how many black bag missions he had conducted in Mexico and South America. Learning the language had been an operational necessity.

"My wife says maybe *senorita* Lizzy went for a walk,

the way Luisa and her used to. She says they liked the woods. The…the…how you say? *Qual es?* The silence. The solitude."

"Okay," Stone said. "Any idea where?"

"*Si*. Yes." Alberto nodded. "They liked the woods where the car was discovered."

Stone's eyes narrowed. How did the Valdezes know about the car Dale had reported? An abandoned vehicle wasn't exactly front page news, even in a small town like Whisper Falls. He remembered Lizzy's story about Alberto's confrontation with Scooby outside of Sloane's Emporium.

Stone said, "Lizzy mentioned you took a job driving. That right?"

Alberto hesitated a long time before answering. "No," he said, then shook his head violently, as if angry with himself. "Yes. *Si*, yes, I did one or two driving jobs. Like delivery driver."

"You're not doing it anymore?"

"No, *senor*."

"Who were you working for?"

"A local businessman. His name is difficult to pronounce. Starts with an 'S' or a 'Z,' I think. Something, like, Savior?"

"Xavier?"

"*Si, senor*." Alberto nodded. "That is him."

"What did he have you delivering?"

"Cars. For his…how you say? Stores."

That checked out. Mason Xavier had his hands in a dozen businesses in Garrison County, including auto dealerships. "Why'd you stop working for him?"

"I am not young anymore." Alberto shrugged. "I try to find job where I can work during day."

"So driving for Xavier was a night job?"

"Mostly, *senor*. Yes."

Stone looked over at Holly, whose eyes were glued to her phone as if she could will a text message from Lizzy to come through. "Anything you want to ask, Holly?"

She shook her head silently, never looking up from the screen.

———

Stone and Holly decided she should wait at home in case Lizzy showed up. As they drove down Main Street, he saw the missing pets flyers stapled to the lampposts and wondered if someday soon he would see a similar flyer with Lizzy's face on it. The thought made his heart hurt more than it already did.

As they pulled into the high-school parking lot so Holly could get her car, Stone heard a choked sob from the passenger seat. He glanced over to see Holly with her hand pressed over her mouth.

"What did I do to deserve this?" she said quietly. "I'm a good person. A good mother. Lizzy's a good kid. Why is this happening to us?"

"Deserve has got nothing to do with it," Stone replied. "Bad things happen to good people. That's just the way the world works sometimes."

"Well, this world sucks and God needs to do a better job. No offense."

"None taken."

She climbed out of the Blazer with a weak smile on her lips and fresh tears on her face. Stone's heart ached for her as he watched her get in her car and drive away, but for once he wasn't sorry to see her go.

He needed to be alone for his next stop.

TWENTY-ONE

STONE RETURNED to the house on the hill. When he drove up to the stone column with the speaker at the entrance, he was surprised to hear Mason Xavier answer instead of his assistant Carlton.

"Hello?"

"Mason, it's Stone. I need to talk to you."

"Stone?" Xavier slurred the word. "Of course. Come right up."

The gate rumbled open and Stone drove up to the mansion. Xavier appeared in his bathrobe, hair disheveled, face wreathed in five o'clock shadow. Stone had never seen him looking this rough. He held a glass in his hand and reeked of booze.

"Greetings, sheriff. Or is it preacher today?" Xavier giggled, obviously well under the influence. "Please, come in and enjoy a drink at the ol' saloon."

Stone stepped inside, shut the door behind him, and followed Xavier as he stumbled into the kitchen and immediately began refreshing his glass. It was barely past noon and the richest man in Garrison County was pie-eyed, a serious day-drunk in progress.

"Something wrong?" Stone asked.

"Everything is wonderful." Xavier dumped ice into his glass and killed half his drink in one gulp. With an exaggerated sigh of contentment, he said, "I am unburdened. Set free. Loosed from my ball and chain."

"Not sure what you're talking about, Mason." Stone shifted his Stetson further back on his head.

"The bitch broke up with me." Xavier stumbled over to a chair and sat down with a heavy sigh. "Goddamned little whore. I came home to find all her stuff gone. Not even the courtesy of a note. Just left her house-keys in the ashtray. Her version of a Dear John letter, I suppose. As in, 'Dear John, we're finished, fuck you.'"

Stone was surprised by Xavier's current vulnerability and inebriation. Whisper Falls' most prominent mogul was a man who prioritized taste above most other concerns. Always impeccably groomed, well-dressed, and perfectly accessorized, Xavier was known for expensive cars, pricey watches, and luxurious taste in food and wine.

Yet here he was, reduced to a shambling, booze-soaked wreck by a woman. His carefully-cultivated shields had come down and left him emotionally exposed, just like any other man. Having your trust betrayed by a woman you love is enough to rip the heart out of any guy.

Stone said the only thing he could think to say. "Sorry to hear that."

"Yeah, yeah." Xavier waved dismissively, closed his eyes, and took a drink. "You know what, Stone? Let's not pretend you and I are friends. No, don't argue with me," he said, even though Stone had no intention of arguing with him. "I know it's true. A man such as myself becomes accustomed to the resentment his success provokes."

"It's not your success I resent, Mason."

"Let me finish." He drained his drink and got up to fix another. "You think I'm a shady guy, a crooked entrepreneur. You're not alone. Many people think you have to be crooked to get rich." He paused to belch, tapping his chest with a closed fist as if fighting heart-burn. "But not me. I'm a regular pillar of the community. Do you have any idea how many opportunities I've created for this crappy little town?"

"I've heard."

"Lots," Xavier said. "This town wouldn't be worth spit without me." He toasted Stone clumsily, spilling booze all over the counter before sweeping the glass to his lips and sucking down the alcohol like it was oxygen.

"So you've created jobs? That what you're getting at?"

"Yes, exactly."

"How about jobs for drivers?"

The question caught Xavier off guard. He frowned as he mentally adjusted to the conversational curve-ball.

"Drivers?" Xavier looked confused, and in Stone's opinion, the confusion seemed genuine, not faked. Plus, Xavier was probably too drunk to fake anything. "I don't…I mean…drivers? We hire some for the dealership, I think. But I don't do the hiring at that level. That's what subordinates are for."

"Any of your subordinates hire Alberto Valdez?"

"Valdez…name sounds familiar." Xavier's face lit up with sudden recognition. "Yes, the refugee guy, right? I know who you're talking about. I met him once. Seemed like a nice guy. But no, we didn't hire him to drive for the dealership."

"So, what *was* your involvement with Valdez?"

"Not much, truth be told." Xavier pushed his glass away. It came to rest next to the ashtray where Yvonne had left her keys on top of a pile of cigarette butts.

"Heard about him through Henry Hutt, the property guy, after a Chamber of Commerce meeting. We were standing around afterwards, just chatting, and Hutt mentioned he had put some refugees up in one of his cottages and that the guy was looking for work. So I took Alberto's contact information, thinking maybe I could find something for him." Xavier suddenly looked puzzled. "Hey, is it funny that a guy who rents houses is named Hutt?"

"Not really. Did you ever call Valdez?"

"Yes. Yvonne asked me to."

"And?"

Xavier shrugged. "Not much to tell. Yvonne said she had some projects that needed a driver and asked if I knew anybody. I remembered Valdez and gave her the info. She said she was going to call him."

"So Valdez was working for Yvonne?"

"Apparently so."

"Any idea what she had him doing?"

"No, but whatever it was, he didn't do it very well. She came home one night furious. Said Valdez had royally fucked up. He picked up a car at the border and was supposed to bring it back here to the house, but apparently he abandoned it in the woods."

The car we turned over to the RCMP, Stone thought.

"Yvonne tried calling him after that but he never answered. When I asked about him a few days later, she said the situation had been handled by one of her guys."

"She say who?"

"No, but it's safe to assume it was Darius Etienne. Not like she would call any of her corporate staff at the main Bloo office in Montreal to handle a local driver. No, for the smaller stuff, she uses Darius, a wrangler of sorts, if you will. A trouble-shooter. Drives a black Lotus." He picked up his glass again and raised it in a toast. "He can rot in hell right alongside the bitch he works for."

Stone nodded. "I understand the sentiment. Thanks for the help. Sorry your girl rode out of town on you."

Xavier snorted derisively and waved a hand. "She was a small investment of time and energy, sheriff. A man in my position learns not to sweat the small stuff."

"I suppose not. Thanks again for your time."

"Of course. We may not be friends, but we need not be enemies either."

Might be too late for that, Stone thought, but kept it to himself.

He let himself out and returned to the Blazer. Things were starting to make more sense now. He had more info on Yvonne and would need to look into this Darius guy. Sports cars weren't really all the rage up here in the mountains, but Garrison County was plenty big enough to get lost in, so even a man driving a distinctive car might be difficult to locate.

And if it turned out Darius had something to do with Luisa's murder or Lizzy's disappearance, not even Hell itself would be big enough to hide him from Stone's wrath.

Through the window, Stone saw Mason Xavier resume drinking. Just another poor bastard crying in his whiskey. Money or not, a broken heart makes fools of us all.

He drove down the hill and headed back into town.

————

He had only made it a mile down the road before his cellphone rang. He glanced at the caller ID and immediately whipped the Blazer to the side of the road and slammed the brakes.

It was Lizzy's number.

TWENTY-TWO

ALL SORTS of emotions rolled through Stone, a knotted mess of feelings that he had no time to untangle right now. He took a deep breath and answered the phone.

"Lizzy? That you?"

A long pause on the other end of the line, followed by a distinctly female chuckle.

"How's my favorite sheriff with his rattlesnake Stetson and shit-kicker cowboy boots?"

Stone recognized Yvonne Brossard's voice.

"What are you doing with Lizzy's phone?" he snapped. "Where is she?"

"That's the question of the day, isn't it? But I'm not going to give you the answer. Not yet. We have some things to discuss first."

Stone's heart thundered in his chest, but he kept his voice cool and calm as he said, "Tell me where she is and we can negotiate."

"God, sheriff, you really are a redneck cowboy." Yvonne laughed. "You clearly don't know anything at all about business dealings. First rule of negotiation—never bargain from a position of weakness. And that's the position you're in right now. You are at a complete disadvantage and I hold all the cards."

"Let Lizzy go. She's got nothing to do with this."

"You don't know that, cowboy." Yvonne's voice had a singsong lilt to it, light and teasing. "All you know is that she's gone and you want her back. You, and her mother. Cute little waitress at the diner. She's your girlfriend, right?"

Stone didn't say anything.

"I have something you want, you have something I want," Yvonne said. "I propose a straight-forward exchange."

"What are you talking about?"

"Your department assisted in a vehicle recovery last week. The RCMP took possession. My sources tell me that the car is currently impounded at a CBPS facility just over the border."

"What's that got to do with anything?"

"That car is mine. I want it back."

"You're talking to the wrong guy. You need the Canadian Border Protection Service."

"No, I'm talking to the right guy. Because of the cards I hold."

A pause, then:

"Luke?"

"Lizzy?" His heart hammered.

"Luke, help me! They're going to—"

She screamed, followed by abrupt silence. Stone gritted his teeth in fear and frustration.

"I didn't know you were on a first name basis with the kid." Yvonne was back on the line. "You two must be closer than I thought."

Stone wanted to snarl threats at her but forced himself to remain calm. Letting his more primal emotions off the leash right now wouldn't do anything to help get Lizzy back.

"All right," he said. "You want the car? That's your demand?"

"There's an abandoned gas station off the last exit on I-87 before you get to the border crossing," Yvonne said. "Know the place?"

"I'll find it."

"Have the car delivered there and make sure everyone walks away. Once I have confirmation from my people that the car is back in our possession, Lizzy will be released. Any bullshit games and Lizzy will be the one who pays the price."

"I'll need time to make the arrangements."

"You've got twelve hours."

"That's not enough time."

"Maybe not, but that's what you've got."

Stone didn't waste his breath arguing. "How do I reach you?"

"Just call Lizzy's phone. And sheriff?"

"Yeah?"

"If you don't make the twelve hour deadline, every thirty minutes after that I'm going to cut off one of her fingers and mail it to you. Understand?"

"Yeah." Stone's blood turned to ice and fury nestled in his guts like a cold, hard knot. "I understand."

"Good." Yvonne hung up.

Stone sat on the shoulder of the road for a long minute, processing it all. The only thing he could do was play the hand he'd been dealt. With all the moving parts and variables, it was difficult to predict the outcome. He would do everything he could to get Lizzy back, including praying like hell, but he knew her safe return was not guaranteed.

But he was sure about one thing.

Yvonne Brossard would pay for this. Whether rotting in a prison cell or blown away by Stone's own smoking gun, she would face justice.

TWENTY-THREE

STONE DROVE IMMEDIATELY to Holly's house and went inside. She looked haggard, lost.

"Any news?" she asked.

"You better sit down."

"No!" Holly's voice quivered. "Is my daughter alive or not? I need to know."

"She's alive. I talked to her."

Holly brightened. "You did? She's okay? Let's go get her!"

"She's been kidnapped."

A thousand emotions crossed Holly's face as she stood there. Relief, puzzlement, fear, and eventually, rage.

"The people who took her have made demands." Stone measured his next words carefully. "Holly, we're going to get her back. Come hell or high water, we're getting Lizzy back. But it's going to be a close call. I need you to trust me."

"I do trust you. And I'm coming with you." She grabbed her purse and jacket.

"Holly, listen…"

"Don't argue with me, Luke. Not today."

"This is going to be dangerous."

"I'm not the one in danger. The ones who took my baby are."

————

They drove to the sheriff's station, went into his office, and closed the door. Stone called Captain Chandler but got no answer, so he left a voicemail, feeling frustrated. The clock was ticking and Lizzy's life expectancy shortened with every grain of sand that trickled through the hourglass.

Luckily, Chandler called him back in less than two minutes.

"Hey, sheriff, good to hear from you. Any news on those vehicles we're watching?"

"I don't have the list in front of me, but is one of them a black Lotus?"

"Sure is." Stone could hear Chandler's mouse clicking in the background as he accessed some database. "Black Lotus Evora GT registered to a Darius Etienne of Montreal. We have unconfirmed reports of sightings of that same car with license plates swapped out. We suspect that's how the border crossings are being facilitated."

"What can you tell me about this Darius guy?"

"Darius Etienne is very bad news. Got his start as a street enforcer for a Montreal crime ring and quickly developed a reputation for extreme brutality and violence. Didn't take long before his services were in high demand and he managed to go freelance. The guy's a complete psychopath. Never proven, but word on the street is that he literally skinned a man alive in St. Jerome last year."

Stone decided to keep that grisly detail from Holly. No point in adding to her stress levels. "So it looks like Darius is working for Yvonne Brossard," he said to Chandler.

Holly's eyes widened at the mention of Yvonne's name, but she didn't say anything.

"That tracks, actually," Chandler replied. "Some of the scumbags he gravitates toward overlap with her circle."

"Speaking of scumbags," Stone said, "Yvonne has kidnapped a teenage girl and is holding her for ransom. Remember the car you took out of our woods last week? She wants it back."

"Damn, she escalated quickly. We know she dabbles in some criminal dealings, but kidnapping? Talk going from zero to sixty in no time flat. What's the threat level to the kid?"

Stone glanced at Holly, who was busy chewing her fingernails down to the ragged quick, eyes glistening with barely-contained tears.

"Maximal," he said quietly.

"Shit." There was a long pause. "So she's committed a kidnapping in the United States and is demanding concessions from Canadian law enforcement in exchange for release of her hostage. Damn, Stone, that's diplomatically complicated, with a whole bunch of cross-border politics. I'll have to run it up the chain of command."

"I have twelve hours. Eleven, at this point."

Chandler drew a sharp breath, followed by a curse.

"I know I'm asking a lot," Stone said, "but we need to keep this operation just between the two of us. You work your end, I work my end. No official connection, but with our actions coordinated."

"Tricky, but…what do you have in mind?"

Stone spelled it out for him.

———

"Yvonne Brossard took Lizzy?" Holly's fury radiated off her in waves. Stone felt the angry heat coming from the passenger seat as he turned out of the parking lot and headed toward Yvonne's rental cottage. "We need to talk to Mason Xavier right now."

"She left him." Stone turned down a side street. "I talked to him earlier today. He's a mess."

"Yeah?" Holly held up her thumb and forefinger pressed together. "That's how much I care about Mason Xavier's broken heart."

"Doesn't change the fact that I rattled his cage and there's nothing there." Stone parked just down the street from the cottage. "He's drunk and feeling sorry for himself, but that's it.

"So where are we?"

"Yvonne's renting this place. I want to take a look inside."

"Do you have a search warrant?"

"Sure." Stone patted the Glock 21 pistol holstered on his belt. "Got one right here. Let's go."

They exited the Blazer and approached the cottage. For some reason, Stone felt like it had an air of abandonment. The driveway was empty and the blinds were drawn. Then again, maybe it was all just a ruse. Stone had the distinct feeling that there was somebody here and he had learned long ago to trust his instincts.

"Let's go around back," he said. "I'll find a door or window to break."

"I'd rather break Yvonne's skull," Holly replied.

"If we get the chance, she's all yours."

They circled around to the backyard. As they turned the corner, Stone stopped dead in his tracks.

"Cade?"

Valentine sprawled at the bottom of the back porch steps, unconscious, bleeding from one ear, his wrists and ankles bound with plastic zip-ties. He was dressed in civilian clothes—pressed jeans, leather shoes, tailored blazer—and a bouquet of bright, cheery flowers lay in a crushed mess next to him. Wasn't hard to figure out what happened—he'd come looking for a date with Yvonne and been cold-cocked.

Stone knelt down beside him and gave his shoulder a gentle shake. "C'mon, Cade, wake up."

It took a couple more shakes, but Valentine finally let out a long, painful moan and cracked open an eye. "Sheriff? That you?"

"What happened?" Stone asked, using his Benchmade folding knife to cut the plastic bindings. Holly knelt down beside the deputy and dabbed at the blood on his neck with a tissue.

Valentine pushed himself up into a sitting position. "Thought I'd drop by and take Yvonne out for lunch. She kept ignoring my texts so I came over in person. Next thing I know—"

A crash from inside the house interrupted him.

Stone rose to his feet, drew his Glock, and ghosted up the stairs onto the back porch. He tried the door handle. It wasn't locked.

Holly tried to follow Stone but he waved her back. She clenched her fists unhappily but complied.

She really wants to hurt someone, Stone thought.

He couldn't blame her.

He eased open the door, which led into the kitchen. Voices inside, male. Sounded like two of them. They were talking low. Not in the kitchen but a different room. Stone strained to hear them. A tracery of words, like bits of a broken cobweb, drifted out to him. Stone detected a French accent.

Gun at the ready, finger on the trigger, he moved into the kitchen, sticking close to the wall.

Clean counters, scrubbed floor, chairs arranged neatly around the dining room table. Someone had tidied up the place for the next renters. The kitchen flowed into a narrow hallway that ran arrow-straight toward the front rooms of the cottage. Doors lined the hall on the left, presumably leading to bedrooms and a bathroom. The front door was in the middle of the hall on the right.

More thumping noises. Voices. Conversational, not alarmed. The sound of items being moved around.

Firmly gripping his Glock, Stone hugged the wall and edged up to the entrance of the hallway. He paused there, waiting and listening. He could hear his own heartbeat in the quiet.

Footsteps in the hall, coming his way. Stone backed up a few feet and raised his pistol. The footsteps paused around the corner, just out of sight.

Two men, speaking French. This close, Stone had no trouble hearing what they were saying. One of them said something about packing a suitcase and the other made a crude joke about sniffing Yvonne's panties. They both laughed and the footsteps resumed. One heading for the front door while the other stepped into the kitchen, a suitcase in each hand.

Stone heard the front door open and then the suitcase guy turned his head and saw Stone standing there with his Glock raised. The man opened his mouth to shout a warning but Stone pistol-whipped him across the jaw. The gun barrel cracked against bone and the guy dropped to the floor.

From outside came a shriek of pain.

Stone left the man crumpled on the kitchen floor. He

moved quickly down the hall, Glock back in a shooting position, and yanked open the front door.

Holly lurked outside, blood dripping from a knife in her fist. Valentine stood nearby, still unsteady, swaying slightly from the blow to the head. The other man who had been in the house was now slumped on the bottom step of the porch. He shrieked again and Stone saw why.

Blood pulsed from slashed flesh and torn tendons as the man tried to hold together what remained of his left ankle.

Holly lunged forward. Grabbed a handful of the man's hair. Yanked his head back. Pressed the knife to his throat, point dimpling the skin.

"Where's my daughter?" she hissed. "Tell me where she is right now!"

The man tried to pull back from her, eyes bugging out of his head as he sputtered in French. But Holly kept his hair locked firmly in her fist, her snarling face inches from his. She increased the pressure on the blade. A bead of blood burst to the surface and trickled down the man's neck like a shaving cut.

Stone moved down beside her. He needed to intervene before she murdered the guy in cold blood on the front porch.

"Holly, back away."

"Dammit, Luke, this son of a bitch knows where Lizzy is!"

"You don't know that yet, but even if he does, we can't cut him to pieces out here for all the neighbors to see." He pulled out his handcuffs and tossed them to Valentine. "Cade, go inside and cuff up the guy in the kitchen. We'll be right behind you with this asshole."

"Copy that." Valentine went up the steps and into the cottage. Stone reached down and hauled the man with the slashed ankle to his feet.

Holly's eyes flashed hotly. "He doesn't get so much as a Band-Aid until he tells me where Lizzy is."

"One step at a time." Stone dragged the guy toward the front door. "And right now the next step is to have a little chat."

TWENTY-FOUR

THEY GATHERED IN THE KITCHEN, the two men sitting in chairs with their hands cuffed behind them.

Despite Holly's protests, Valentine found a first aid kit and tended to the man's savaged ankle while the other guy groggily came awake and tried to shake off the effects of Stone's pistol-whipping.

The suitcases Ankle Man had been carrying sat in the corner. Stone had found boxes of personal items stacked in the living room, awaiting transport. It looked like Ankle Man and Pistol Whip were Yvonne's lackeys, sent to pack up her belongings.

Holly paced angrily up and down the hallway, feet stomping like hammers. Her rage was omnipresent, filling the entire house, boiling off her in endless waves.

"Time to talk," Stone said, arms folded across his chest, hip braced against the kitchen table as he stared at the two men. "Just so we're clear, this won't be friendly. I'm going to ask some questions and you're going to answer them."

"The hell we will!" Pistol Whip snarled. "Read us our

rights, give us our goddamn phone calls, and then eat shit, asshole."

"You're off to a bad start." Stone uncrossed his arms and slammed a fist into the guy's mouth, crushing his lips against his teeth. "You're not the one in charge here, I am. And I really don't appreciate you telling me what to do."

Pistol Whip leaned forward in his chair and spat blood on the floor. He sat back up and glared at Stone. "I know the law and I know my rights."

"I smashed your face in with my gun," Stone said, then gestured at Holly. "She carved your friend's ankle open with a knife. You're currently handcuffed in a goddamned kitchen. Do you really think I give a damn about your rights?"

"I'm not scared of you."

"You should be." Stone smiled coldly. "To get Lizzy Bennet back, I'm willing to do things that would make the devil throw up."

Pistol Whip's face paled as the toughness drained out of him like blood from a slit vein. He glanced around the room as if seeking help from one of the others, but Valentine just stared at him grimly and Holly looked like she wanted to rip his throat out with her bare teeth. Stone had no doubt that if he told her to, she would do just that.

"Cade," Stone said to his deputy, "things are about to get ugly. If you want to walk away, now's the time."

"Screw that," Valentine replied. "These scumbags ambushed me and knocked me out. I'm perfectly okay with them feeling some pain."

"Pain?" Stone leveled his gaze at the deputy. "Before this is over, I might very well kill them."

Valentine stared at him, saw the seriousness in his eyes, and swallowed hard. "That...that's murder, sheriff."

"Better them than Lizzy. Like I said, walk away."

Valentine squared his shoulders. "No. A kid's life is at stake. We do what we have to do."

"Doing it's the easy part," Stone said softly. "Living with it is what's hard."

Without warning, he slammed a punch into Pistol Whip's jaw, targeting the flesh and bone already bruised by the gun barrel. The blow snapped the man's head around so fast that a rope of bloody spittle flew from his mouth and splattered on the kitchen table.

Stone walked over to the other guy and kicked him in his wounded ankle. The man howled in pain.

"First one to talk gets to live," Stone said. "Where's Yvonne?"

Ankle Man looked terrified. His pain-filled eyes were huge saucers set in the swarthiness of his face.

Stone took out his knife and flicked it open. "Normally when I'm conducting an interrogation like this, I just shoot people in various body parts until they talk. But I don't want the neighbors to be disturbed by any gunshots, so I'm going to start cutting instead. By the time I get to your balls, one of you bastards will tell me what I want to know."

A slow stain spread across the front of Ankle Man's jeans as he pissed himself.

Stone knew his warrior side had taken over. The preacher who stood behind the pulpit on Sunday mornings and proclaimed Christ's love was now threatening to castrate a man. For the time being, his fury had eclipsed his faith. When this was over, he would need to learn how to strike a better balance.

Easier said than done, he thought.

Right now, fear and rage sizzled through his veins over Lizzy's abduction. When she was safe, he would have a talk with God about doing a better job of controlling his more primal impulses.

But that would have to wait. Right now…

Stone drove the knife into Ankle Man's leg, just above the kneecap, with enough force to hit bone. He took no pleasure in the torture, forcing himself to remain cold and dispassionate. It was just something that needed to be done, a savage means to a necessary end, not something to be relished.

He left the blade sticking out of Ankle Man's leg and said, "Tell me where Yvonne Brossard is."

A groan of pain escaped from between the guy's clenched teeth and beads of sweat exploded across his forehead. The two Frenchman exchanged desperate looks but neither of them said anything.

"Trust me, boys, silence is not an option. You're either going to talk or you're going to scream."

Holly suddenly stormed out of the hallway, chest heaving, teeth gritted. The look in her eyes reminded Stone of a wild horse getting roped for the first time. Furious. Desperate. And more than a little bit crazy. She grabbed the knife stuck in Ankle Man's leg and twisted.

"Where is she?" she demanded. "Where's my baby girl?" Her enraged voice filled the room, pained and haunting.

The man screamed as the sharp metal corkscrewed open his flesh. But no words, no answers, came out of his mouth.

Stone pulled Holly away. "Enough."

"It's not enough until he tells me where she is." She spun around and headed back down the hall. "I'm going to go find a blowtorch."

As she stomped away, Stone looked at Pistol Whip. "You're running out of time. When she comes back, I'm not going to stop her, no matter what she does to you."

The man cut loose with a stream of profanity in French that steadily increased in volume until the man was shouting, the cords in his neck rigid with stress. Then he abruptly deflated like a pin-pricked balloon, all the resistance draining out of him. "You've got the wrong guys," he said, reverting to English. "We don't even work for Yvonne. At least, not directly."

"Who then?"

"Darius. She gives him the orders, and Darius gives them to us."

"Darius. Her assistant?"

"Yes." Pistol Whip nodded. "That's who we work for. He calls when he has a job for us."

"A job like kidnapping a young girl?"

"We didn't know anything about that."

Stone stared at him, hard and unforgiving. "You're lying. Lie to me again, I'm gonna pull the knife out of your friend's leg and stick it in your guts. Got it?"

Pistol Whip hesitated for a moment, weighing the truth of Stone's words. He must have decided the cowboy meant it, because his next words were, "Okay, we knew about the kidnapping, but we didn't have anything to do with it."

"How about Luisa Valdez? You have anything to do with that?"

"Who?"

"The girl who was burned to death."

"We bought the lighter fluid and gave it to Darius, that's it."

"Did you know what he was planning on doing with it?"

Pistol Whip hesitated again, then said, "Not exactly, but kind of."

"What the hell does that mean?"

"He burned someone alive before, just outside of

Montreal, in Iles-de-Boucherville National Park. He had us buy the lighter fluid for that one too, so we figured the same thing was happening here."

"So you didn't do the killings, you're just an accessory," Stone growled in disgust. "You just stood by and let innocent people die. I should do the world a favor and put a bullet in both your heads."

"We're nobodies," Pistol Whip pleaded. "How do you say it? Gofers. Lackeys. Yeah, that's what we are. Not much better than paid slaves. We do the small work for Darius. Not the killing."

"The blood doesn't wash off your hands that easily," Stone said. "Ask Pontius Pilate."

"Who?"

"Never mind. What's Darius got you doing today? Why are you here?"

"He sent us here to move Yvonne's stuff. Pack it up and ship it back to Montreal. She was staying here, now she's not. That's all I know."

"So you don't know where she is?"

"No."

"How about Darius?"

"He's supposed to meet us here." Pistol Whip glanced at a clock on the wall. "In about twenty minutes. He's got our cash."

"All right." Stone plucked the knife out of Ankle Man's leg, eliciting a fresh gasp of pain. "See how easy that was? Could have saved yourselves some hurt if you had just talked sooner rather than later."

"People who talk about Darius usually don't live too long. He's a bad man."

"Yeah? What do you think I am?"

Pistol Whip looked at the blood on the knife in Stone's hand, then at the hard lines of his face. "You, I think, are both good and bad."

Ain't that the truth, Stone thought. *Or, hell, maybe I'm not good at all.*

"I couldn't find a blowtorch."

Holly walked back into the room, her words somehow both flat and simmering with fury. Her eyes, blazing with cold fire, impaled the two handcuffed men. They both fidgeted nervously under her withering glare.

"You both better pray I get my daughter back unharmed," she said. "Or I swear to God I will walk down to the store, buy a brand new blowtorch, and come back here to burn your eyeballs out of your fucking skulls."

"Hey, now, wait a minute!" Pistol Whip turned to Stone. "We told you everything we know. You can't let her threaten us like that."

"I didn't hear her make any threat," Stone replied. "All I heard was a promise."

————

Stone had Valentine relocate his Chevy Blazer to the next street over so Darius wouldn't see it and get spooked when he arrived. He pulled the curtains in the front room closed, leaving just a crack so he could keep watch.

When Valentine got back, Stone asked him, "You packing, Cade?"

"Just my off-duty piece." Valentine pulled up his pant leg to reveal a Walther PPS pistol strapped to his ankle.

"Better than nothing." Stone double-checked his Glock to make sure there was a round chambered, then slid it back into its holster. "Stay here, keep watch, and give a whistle when Darius shows up."

"Copy that."

Back in the kitchen, Ankle Man and Pistol Whip looked nervous, keeping their eyes on Holly. She leaned on the table and stared at them with a look on her face that would make the devil proud. Stone had seen that look before. It was the look of someone hurting and in a killing mood.

"Hey, man," Ankle Man said. "Don't leave us alone with her again. This *la chienne* is crazy!"

"Her daughter has been kidnapped by the assholes you work for," Stone replied. "You're lucky she doesn't tear you apart with her bare hands."

"We didn't take her daughter!"

Stone shrugged. "Guilt by association."

"What are you going to do with us?"

"Shoot you in the mouth if you don't shut up."

The man started to say something, did a double take at the look on Stone's face, and changed his mind.

Stone pulled Holly close and kept his voice low. "We're going to grab Darius and offer an exchange. Darius plus these two guys for Lizzy."

"Sounds risky."

"It is."

"Luke, this is my daughter we're talking about!"

"I know." He put a hand on her shoulder. "This gives us a shot at getting her back. I think we should take it."

"You're asking me to trust you with Lizzy's life."

"I know what I'm asking."

Holly looked like she wanted to object. Stone could see her weighing everything in her mind. This had to be hell on her. Given the circumstances, she was holding it together remarkably well. Probably better than he would have if he was in her shoes.

A whistle came from the front room.

"Show time," Stone said. "Stay out of sight." He trotted over to the window and joined Valentine at the curtain.

Outside, the throaty rumble of a high-performance

engine approached the cottage. Stone drew his Glock as Darius' Lotus appeared on the street, slowing to a stop in front of the house. The taillights flashed red and stayed that way as Darius didn't shift into park but just sat there idling with his foot on the brake. Due to the tinted glass, the enforcer wasn't much more than a shadow behind the wheel. But you could practically feel the menace oozing from the car like exhaust smoke.

"He's casing the joint," Valentine muttered. "He knows something's wrong."

"There's no way he can know that."

"Criminals have a sixth sense about this kind of thing," Valentine replied. "I've seen it, you've seen it."

Stone knew Valentine was right. His pulse quickened as he waited for Darius to get out of the car. *Come on, you bastard. What are you waiting for?*

He would never know the answer to that question. After lingering for a full minute, Darius punched the gas and the car peeled off down the street.

TWENTY-FIVE

HOLLY WAS STILL TREMBLING with anger when Stone pulled into the sheriff's station parking lot a short time later.

"I can't believe you just let him go."

"I didn't have a choice." Stone switched off the ignition.

"We could have grabbed him!"

"Not without a car chase, and that would have given him time to call Yvonne and tell her to kill Lizzy."

The words got her attention like a hard slap to the face. She inhaled sharply and squeezed her eyes shut, as if hoping that when she opened them again, this would all turn out to be a nightmare from which she could awaken. A single tear escaped to bleed down her cheek.

"What are we going to do?" she whispered.

"We're going to set a trap."

As if on cue, his cell phone buzzed as a call from Captain Chandler came through. He answered it immediately.

"This is Stone."

Chandler didn't waste time with small talk. "It took

some doing, but I've arranged to 'borrow' that suspect vehicle tonight. But if it's not back where it belongs by noon tomorrow, my butt's in a sling."

"This will all be over by noon tomorrow," Stone said. *One way or the other,* he silently added.

"My people will arrange to get the car across the border," Chandler continued. "I'm only using guys I totally trust on this one."

Stone was impressed. Canadian law enforcement's reputation was generally cordial but slow. Chandler was taking a big risk cutting through the tangled red tape of government bureaucracy. He was putting his career on the line and would be looking for a new job if this covert action turned into a pooch-screw. It reminded Stone that there were still good men left in the world.

"We need the car parked at an abandoned gas station off the last exit on I-87 before the border," Stone said. "My guess is that Yvonne will send some boys to pick it up."

"It'll be there. Hope you get the girl back."

"From your lips to God's ears."

"Good luck, Stone."

Stone hung up and Holly stared at him. She trembled, probably from a volatile mix of fear and rage. She reminded Stone of a caged lioness whose cubs have been threatened.

"The car Yvonne wants will be in position," Stone told her. "I'm sure she'll have people in place, watching. Once she has the car in her possession, she'll contact us to arrange a meeting to give Lizzy back."

"And then what? You'll arrest her?"

"I was thinking something more permanent," Stone said grimly.

———

It was all a waiting game now, sand slipping through the hourglass in painfully slow motion. Stone offered to drive Holly home but she refused. She paced in his office, back and forth, threatening to wear a groove in the hardwood floor.

The clock moved sluggishly, each tick forward seeming to take sixty minutes instead of sixty seconds. Whisper Falls was not a town where time moved fast on a regular day. Today, with Lizzy's life hanging in the balance, it seemed to be moving slower than a tortoise crawling uphill through cold molasses.

When Chief Fox called, Stone welcomed the diversion. Talking about the arson investigation would distract him for a few minutes from thinking about Lizzy.

"Hey, chief," he greeted. "I know you left me a couple messages. Sorry I didn't get back to you. We've got a situation here."

"Heard about that," Fox said. "No need to apologize. A missing girl takes precedent over anything else. I just wanted to let you know that Vince Gunther is missing."

"What do you mean, missing?"

"I'm at the apartment building he was staying at. I think you should come see for yourself."

First Lizzy abducted and now Vince Gunther missing? Stone couldn't imagine the two were related. But stranger things had happened and he knew he still didn't have all the pieces to this particular puzzle. Besides, they were just sitting here doing nothing, so he had time to spare. The apartment building was less than a mile away, so this wouldn't take long. Stop by, talk to Fox, and then come right back here to resume watching the clock crawl.

He said, "I'll be there in five."

"What are we doing?" Holly's tone from the passenger seat made it clear she was upset. "We need to be focused on getting Lizzy back, not Vince Gunther."

"This won't take long," Stone said. "And let's face it, all we're doing right now is waiting, so we've got the time."

This seemed to mollify her. Stone turned onto Park Street and found the red, three-story apartment building —a renovated tuberculosis "cure house"—down at the end before the road made a ninety-degree curve and dropped down the hill toward the old railroad tracks. He pulled into the driveway, directly behind Fox's truck.

"Wait here," he said to Holly, who nodded.

He found Fox out back, standing near the cellar entryway that led to the one-bedroom basement apartment where Gunther had been staying. The building itself contained five apartment units: one on the main floor, two on the second story, an upstairs loft for anyone willing to carry their groceries up three flights of stairs, and this basement unit. Stone knew at least one person who lived here—Tom 'Raff' Rafferty. The loss prevention specialist rented the first floor apartment.

"Afternoon, sheriff," Fox greeted. "Thanks for coming. I know you've got other business, so I'll cut right to the chase. You have any idea where Vince Gunther might be?"

"Last I knew, he was living here."

"Not anymore." Fox motioned for Stone to follow him into the basement. Across from a utility room with a bank of coin-operated washing machines and dryers, the door to the rental unit was open. Fox gestured inside. "See for yourself."

Stone entered the apartment. Even if his eyes were closed, he would have been able to tell the place was empty. It just had that air about it, a vibe of abandonment.

Where the hell are you, Vince?

The floor of the apartment was covered with indoor/outdoor carpeting that was a bright green color just one shade shy of qualifying as neon. That eyesore carpet alone would have been enough to make Stone not want to live here.

The kitchenette was spotless, not a dish or food container anywhere to be found. The refrigerator was empty and unplugged. Sticking his head in the closet-sized bathroom, Stone saw the medicine cabinet open, the shelves cleaned out.

In the bedroom, the bed was unmade and the dresser drawers were open, empty. It looked like Vince had packed up and left in a hurry. Stone did another quick scan of the place and then rejoined Fox, who had moved back outside into the yard.

"Yeah, looks like he's gone."

"Any idea why he bailed out?" Fox asked. "Or where he went?"

Stone shook his head. "No. But follow me." He walked back around to the front of the house, up onto the porch, into the foyer, and knocked on a door at the end of a short hallway.

He heard feet shuffling inside and a moment later the door swung open. Raff stood there in a flannel robe and moccasin-style slippers, a Coors Light in his hand. The sound of a football game floated out from another room. "Hey, sheriff. What brings you here?"

"Business, Raff. You got a second?"

"Sure." Raff stepped out into the hall and closed the door behind him. "What's up?"

"You know Vince Gunther? The guy living downstairs?"

"The guy who *was* living downstairs, you mean." Raff paused to take a swig of beer. "He's the gentleman whose wife died in the fire, right? Moved in here right after that but didn't stay long. He vacated the premises yesterday."

"Did you see him leave?"

"Hard to miss," Raff said. "I had just gotten back from a shift at Sloane's. Heard him banging around downstairs. Back and forth to his pickup truck with boxes and suitcases. Seemed to be in a real hurry."

"Any idea why?"

Raff shook his head. "He just loaded up his crap, slammed the tailgate, and hauled ass outta here lickety-split. Almost like he was being chased."

What are you running from, Vince? Stone wondered, but kept the thought to himself.

"Thanks, Raff."

"No problem, sheriff."

Back out on the porch, Stone looked at Fox. "Sounds like he hit the road to God knows where. I'll put out a BOLO." He glanced over at the Blazer. Holly looked like she was getting restless. "Best I can do right now."

"Appreciate it, Stone." Fox shook his hand. "Now go get that girl back."

———

Holly was nearly chewing the dashboard when Stone climbed back into the Blazer. She verbally pounced on him immediately.

"Luke, you mind telling me how the hell this is helping get Lizzy back?"

He turned the key in the ignition, listened to the engine rumble to life, and then turned to her. "Holly, we're getting Lizzy back. We're complying with Yvonne's demands. All we can do now it wait for her to call."

Holly didn't respond. She just stared at Stone, jaw clenched as she struggled to control her emotions. She closed her eyes and a single tear slid down her cheek like a drop of liquid silver.

"God, Luke, I've never been so scared in my entire life," she whispered.

Stone's heart ached for her. Holly was one hell of a woman—proud, strong, hardworking, devoted to her daughter—and it pained him to see her in so much anguish. Lizzy's abduction had reduced Holly to a raw husk humming with rage and fear and adrenaline. Stone wondered how much longer she could hold it together.

"I know." He reached over and put a comforting hand on her shoulder. "She's your baby girl. We'll get her back and then Yvonne and her crew will pay for what they did. I swear to God, Holly, they're going to pay."

"Make sure they do, Luke." Her eyes were still closed, as if in prayer. "Please, God, make them pay."

Amen, Stone thought.

TWENTY-SIX

"THOSE TWO IDIOTS SURE ARE DUMB." Valentine sighed as he closed the door of the interview room. "I'm surprised Yvonne would hire them to scrub her toilet, let alone pick up her stuff."

Stone felt frustrated. He had hoped the two men—or at least one of them—would have some insight into Yvonne's current location. That would have given him a chance to go on the offensive instead of sitting around waiting for her to call. But the two lackeys had proven to be useless.

"Where did you put her stuff?" he asked Valentine.

"Evidence room."

"Thanks."

Stone went down the hall, glancing into his office on the way by. Holly was asleep in his chair where she'd collapsed after a crying jag. Stone switched off the lights and shut the door so she wouldn't be disturbed. Some rest would do her good.

Yvonne Brossard's suitcases and boxes of belongings were piled in the evidence room. None of the contents had been catalogued yet; that was a task for another day.

Stone looked everything over and his eyes settled on a backpack-style laptop carrier sitting on the sorting table.

He dragged it over by the strap, opened the zipper, and pulled out the computer nestled inside. He figured Yvonne, like most business people, would rely on her phone and laptop the way most persons rely on their internal organs to keep them alive. Running a business, especially a successful one like Bloo, required meticulous recordkeeping of all transactions, meeting arrangements, and agreements.

Which meant there would be a digital trail to follow.

The laptop was a cutting-edge, top-of-the-line product. But in the end, a laptop was just a laptop. Stone flipped it open and powered up the screen.

Naturally, the computer was password-protected. But a quick call to a hacker buddy from his warrior days who owed him a favor after Stone saved his life during a mission in Somalia took care of that problem. The guy remoted in and cracked the encryption in less than three minutes.

"Next time you call, give me a challenge," he said. "I know second graders who could have done this."

"Thanks for the help," Stone replied. "I owe you one."

"You don't owe me a damn thing. It's the other way around."

They said their goodbyes and Stone buckled down to examining the contents of the laptop. He would take any edge he could get over Yvonne Brossard.

Her background picture was a nocturnal shot of a city skyline. Probably Montreal if he had to guess. He started clicking his way through her folders, scanning the information they contained.

The most recent files revealed text documents, emails, and spreadsheets. Nothing too interesting there, but he found a subfolder simply titled "NY." He opened it and found an accounting ledger.

His eyes narrowed as he studied the columns. Names and numbers and dollar amounts. One of the names jumped out at him. It had a line struck through it.

~~Valdez~~.

There was no dollar amount next to the name, just red X's.

Stone took off his Stetson and ran his fingers through his hair. He couldn't be sure what it all meant, but it was another piece of a puzzle that was starting to come together.

Cars running back and forth across the border, one of them tied to gang violence in Toronto. Scooby working for Yvonne. A series of fires ripping through Whisper Falls and the surrounding county. And worst of all, Luisa Valdez murdered in cold blood, literally burned to death.

When you put those facts together with all the other random puzzle pieces, the logical answer was drugs. It was the simplest explanation.

Stone was willing to bet that was the reason Yvonne wanted the car back so badly. The seats and panels were probably loaded with hidden contraband and even though the vehicle had been in police custody, he doubted the RCMP had disassembled it or bothered to have a K-9 give it a sniff. The car was connected to a murder, not narcotics.

So when Yvonne got her car back, she would get her drugs back as well. Frankly, Stone didn't really give a damn, as long as she released Lizzy unharmed.

He turned his attention to the emails. Most of it was boring business drivel, but one of the messages was from a name Stone recognized, a realtor in north Garrison County. He double-clicked to read the contents.

Ms. Brossard:

Thank you so much for choosing Demer Properties for your rental needs! We're pleased that the office complex on North Waterford Road is suited to your requirements.

North Waterford Road was located on the northern fringe of Garrison County, not too far from the Canadian border. A gated access road led to a corporate office complex that had been built by a software firm back in the early '90s and abandoned around 2012. But it was still in good shape and a $4 million dollar asking price reflected that. Based on the email, Yvonne was just renting the complex, but even that couldn't be cheap.

But if she was smuggling drugs over the border, she would need a place to stage her operation, and the North Waterford complex—large, gated, and remote—was perfect for that. He made a mental note to investigate further once they had Lizzy back.

It was just past midnight. Yvonne should be calling any minute now. Stone left the evidence room and walked to the front of the station. Catfish was running night duty but he wasn't alone like he would normally be. Valentine and Drummond were both present, ready to back up Stone.

"Thanks for coming, guys," Stone said. "Should be any minute now, so be ready to roll."

"Wouldn't miss it for the world," said Valentine.

Drummond patted the Remington 870 shotgun laying on his desk. "Just let me get that evil bitch in my sights and she's going down."

"Shoot to kill, sheriff?" Valentine asked.

"We do whatever it takes to get Lizzy back," Stone replied. "After that…"

He didn't finish the thought. His code of primal justice meant he would gun down Yvonne Brossard without batting an eye. But his deputies were lawmen and he would not ask them to violate their oath.

Drummond grinned at him. "You know, for a preacher, you sure can be awfully damn bloodthirsty sometimes."

"It's the Eleventh Commandment," Stone said. "Thou shalt not fuck with people I care about."

Over at the front desk, Catfish called out, "Whatever Bible you're reading, I need to get me a copy."

Stone went back to his office and crouched down beside Holly, his features softening as he studied her sleeping face. She seemed so at peace right now that he hated to wake her up and bring her back to hellish reality.

He stayed that way for several minutes, then reached out and gently shook her awake. "Hey."

Holly's eyes opened. She took a deep breath that turned into a yawn, then sat up in the chair. "Has she called yet?"

"Not yet. Want a cup of coffee?"

"The only thing I want is my daughter back."

Her words came out a little sharper than she had probably intended, but Stone easily let it go. She was under more stress than he could possibly imagine. Sure, he had lost a daughter, but it had happened quickly, without warning. Holly had to suffer endless hours knowing her daughter was in the clutches of a woman savage enough to order an innocent girl burned alive and a man brutal enough to flay the flesh off his victims.

His cellphone rang at 12:36 a.m. It was Lizzy's number.

Holly stared at the phone with eyes full of both hope and hate. The conflicting emotions would have been unnerving if Stone didn't understand exactly how she felt.

He answered the call, putting the phone on speaker.

"This is Stone."

"Howdy, cowboy." Yvonne chuckled. "Still got some of that Wild West swagger left or has it all gone out the window now that you're holding the losing hand?"

Stone clenched his jaw. "This isn't about winning or losing. This is about getting Lizzy back. Nothing else matters."

"My people inform me the car was left at the proper location and is now back in our possession. You kept up your end of the bargain. Consider me impressed. I seriously had my doubts you would be able to pull it off. The Mounties must owe you some favors."

"I got it done. The details don't matter."

"You really do get off on being a man of few words," Yvonne said. "That shit-kicker silence isn't as charming as you seem to think it is."

"I'll talk all you want after you give Lizzy back."

"Fine," Yvonne sighed. "You can have the bitch back. High school parking lot, twenty minutes."

"We'll be there."

"Bring my personal belongings with you—everything you stole from my rental house. I want it all back."

With Lizzy's life at stake, Stone wasn't going to argue with her. "You can have it."

"Keep the faith, cowboy. If all goes well, this will be over soon."

"Yvonne, this is Holly Bennett."

Holly's voice was soft, menacing, and colder than a graveyard on a winter's night. It was like her words were encased in ice.

"Hello, Holly." Yvonne's tone was taunting. "Your daughter is having a wonderful time. She's taken a real *hardcore* interest in Darius, if you know what I mean. Or maybe it's the other way around. Anyway, she really wishes you were here."

"I *will* be there," Holly replied, her voice eerily calm.

"Then I'll see you soon, I guess. Looking forward to it."

"I just want to make one thing clear—if anything happens to my daughter, I'll kill you."

TWENTY-SEVEN

THEY DROVE along the darkened road to the high school in silence. Holly stared out the passenger window, her reflection mirrored in the glass. She wore a calm, almost blank expression on her face that was more frightening than the fear and rage she had exhibited all day.

Stone maintained radio silence but he knew his deputies were deployed near the school. Valentine was stationed just off a side road near the football field, his squad car tucked back in an old junkyard for concealment. He had dropped Drummond off earlier so the senior deputy could approach through the woods behind the school.

Stone shot a glance over at Holly. "Your Jeep is still at the school, right?"

She nodded.

"Okay," he said. "As soon as you have Lizzy, put her in your car and go straight back to the station. Catfish will be waiting for you."

Holly didn't say anything, just kept staring out the window. She seemed a little shell-shocked, which wasn't exactly unexpected. Stone was just about ready to repeat his instructions when she finally responded.

"We've been through so much, Luke." She sounded tired, the kind of weariness that burrows straight down past the bone and into the soul. "The abuse from my ex-husband. Getting jerked around by Witness Protection. Those scumbag survivalists last year. And now this." She paused long enough to swallow a lump in her throat. "If anything happens to Lizzy…"

"Nothing is going to happen. We're going to get Lizzy back and then deal with Yvonne and Darius. Simple as that."

Thing was, Stone wasn't sure whether he was trying to assure Holly…or himself.

———

As they pulled into the main parking of the high school, Stone's radio crackled to life. "Drummond to Stone, come in."

Stone plucked the mike from its dashboard cradle. "Go ahead."

"We've got company. There's a car posted up near the woods behind the school."

Stone silently cursed. It wasn't unexpected that Yvonne would bring reinforcements, but he had hoped she and Darius would come alone. Looked like Lady Luck wasn't riding shotgun tonight.

"Have they spotted you?" Stone asked.

"Not sure. It's possible."

"Keep an eye on them and watch your six."

"Copy that."

The parking lot was dark. By day, the campus crawled with kids getting an education, learning, socializing, playing. But tonight, a much deadlier game was being played.

As Stone swung the Blazer into the parking lot, head-lights flashed at the far end—once, twice—and then went dark again.

Game time, Stone thought. *Hang on, Lizzy. Almost there.*

He saw the outline of two vehicles—one low slung, and the other apparently some kind of SUV. He figured the low slung one was Darius' Lotus and the other one belonged to Yvonne.

Stone pulled up next to Holly's Jeep Gladiator. He kept the engine running as she got out and started the vehicle. He could see her squinting through the windshield, desperately straining for a sight of her daughter. He mentally urged her to stay cool. Now was not the time for recklessness.

He took a deep breath, opened the door, and stepped out.

The headlights on both the Lotus and the SUV blossomed, haloing the area in a corona of harsh light. Stone lowered his Stetson to shield his eyes from the glare. Holly exited her Jeep and stood beside him.

The Lotus' driver-side door opened and a slender figure emerged. Stone couldn't be sure but he assumed it was Darius. The dual pair of high beams made it difficult to see any details. But he could see well enough to glimpse the pistol in the man's hand.

"Drop your gun, sheriff," Darius ordered. "Do it now. You even think about playing hero, Yvonne will slit the girl's throat."

Stone did as instructed. He slowly pulled his Glock 21 from the holster and set it down on the pavement.

"Backup piece, too," Darius commanded. "And don't tell me you don't have one. No cop worth his salt only carries one gun."

Stone hesitated but only for a fraction of a second. Until Lizzy was released, Darius and Yvonne called the shots. He reached into the pocket of his rancher coat, took out the Colt Cobra .38 revolver, and placed it on the ground next to the Glock.

"Kick them away," Darius said.

Stone used his boot to send the pistols skating across the pavement into the darkness beyond the range of the headlights.

"Good boy," Darius taunted.

"Let me see Lizzy," Stone said. "I need proof of life."

"Une moment, mon ami." Darius' voice was mocking. "This ends when we decide, not you."

"Where is she?" Holly asked, her tone calm but chilly. "I want to see my daughter." A few seconds passed before she added through clenched teeth, "Please."

"Relax, mom." Darius moved forward into the light, revealing a mocking grin that Stone wanted to wipe off his face, preferably with buckshot. "Your baby is right here. You just need to remember who's in charge."

Stone recognized Darius' desire to assert control of the situation, sensed the invisible tendrils of dominance flexing in the air around them. He refused to react to it, knowing that Drummond and Valentine were out there in the darkness, backing him up. Right now, remaining cool, calm, and patient was the right play.

"The car was left where you wanted it," Stone said. "Time to honor your end of the bargain."

"When we're goddamned good and ready."

As if on cue, the door of the SUV opened and two shapes emerged, nothing more than blurred shadows behind the blast of the headlights. But despite not being able to get a good look at them, Stone had no doubt that it was Lizzy and Yvonne.

Stone could sense Holly straining beside him,

yearning to rush forward and gather Lizzy into her arms, but she somehow managed to control herself.

Stone yearned to protect Lizzy as well, but he also yearned to put a bullet through Yvonne's heart. Justice or vengeance, he wasn't sure which, nor did he care. He firmly believed that some people just deserved to die and Yvonne Brossard was one of them. Her beauty masked an evil soul.

"Lizzy?" The name exploded desperately from Holly's lips. "Lizzy, is that you?"

"Mom?" Lizzy sounded scared. "Mom, I'm—"

Yvonne's hand moved in a blur. The harsh crack of flesh striking flesh whiplashed through the night and Lizzy stopped talking. Stone felt his rage intensify. Felt the same red-hot emotions from Holly. Her civilized veneer cracked and a deep, low growl rose from within her, inaudible to anyone but Stone.

She's about to go feral, Stone thought, praying she could hold it together just a little bit longer.

"Well, isn't this nice?" Yvonne stepped into the light, her hand twisted in Lizzy's hair. Lizzy's eyes, wide and terrified, reminded Stone of a horse trapped in a barn fire.

Stone hated to see her like that. She'd already been through so much in her young life. This would be yet another scar on her psyche that she would have to somehow learn to live with.

Of course, first she just had to live.

"Mother and child reunited, just like a fucking Disney movie." Yvonne sneered. "Just remember, cowboy, we've got the upper hand here."

"Tell me something," Stone said. "How do you plan to get away with this? Every cop between here and the border will be hunting for you. That's not the upper hand, that's a suicide run."

Yvonne smiled. "We have a contingency plan."

Stone heard a pair of footsteps approaching in the dark behind Darius. A moment later Drummond appeared in the circle of light, shoved along by Scooby. Bruises covered the deputy's face and his clothing was disheveled. He'd clearly come out on the wrong side of a beating.

Scooby halted beside Darius and tucked the muzzle of a pistol directly behind Drummond's ear. One pull of the trigger and it would be raining brain tissue.

The deputy looked embarrassed. "Sorry, sheriff. Bastard got the drop on me."

"You all right?"

"Nothing an icepack and couple shots of whiskey won't cure." Drummond took a deep breath, then exhaled long and slow. "Just get this punk-ass son of a bitch to drop his gun and I'll show him how fast an old cop can move."

Stone nodded. His senior deputy was made out of rawhide and leather. It would take more than a beat-down to break his fighting spirit. Stone mentally added the beating to the long list of things Yvonne and Darius needed to pay for.

"So," Yvonne said, "we've got one deputy and one little girl." She jerked her hand in Lizzy's hair, causing her to whimper. "You play it our way, cowboy, or nobody goes home alive."

Stone glanced at Holly to see how she was taking it. She stood motionless, almost as if hypnotized. Her eyes blazed hot as she stared at Yvonne like she wanted to rip out the woman's throat with her bare teeth.

Darius' phone rang. Stone felt his pulse quicken. He took a deep breath to force it back under control.

"*Allo?*" Darius held the phone to his ear, listening. Then he nodded and said, "*C'est bon. D'accord.*" He hung up and turned to Yvonne. "The car is back across the border. We're good."

"Very good." She smiled, the gesture both sweet and wicked at the same time. "I love it when a plan comes together. Sheriff, it's been a pleasure working with you."

"Stay the hell out of Garrison County," Stone rasped. "Don't ever come back to my town again."

"Or what?" Yvonne smirked.

"Or you'll leave in a pine box."

"Is that a threat, cowboy? Or just a promise?"

"Both." Stone took a step forward. "Now let Lizzy go."

Yvonne looked like she might be ready to comply, then Darius' phone rang again. She looked over at her right-hand man, eyes narrowed, and Stone got the distinct feeling things had just gone right to hell.

"Hello?" Darius answered in English this time. He listened for a moment, swallowed hard, and then hung up and turned to Yvonne. "Mounties ambushed them right after they crossed the border. They're trying to get away but it's not looking good."

"Fuck!" Yvonne screamed.

Three things happened in rapid succession.

Drummond twisted away from Scooby's pistol and threw an elbow up and back into the junkie's jaw. It hit with a satisfying crack and Scooby went all wobbly and dropped to the ground. The gun fell forgotten from his hand.

Yvonne dragged Lizzy back into the SUV.

Darius leveled his pistol at Stone and fired.

Stone's combat-honed reflexes saved him. Anticipating Darius' action, he was on the move before the shot left the muzzle. He threw himself to the side, in the direction of the guns he had kicked away. The bullet ripped through the space he had occupied a heartbeat before.

Darius didn't bother with any follow-up shots. He dove into the Lotus, intent on hauling ass out of there. The SUV and the Lotus both surged forward.

"Lizzy!"

Stone heard Holly's panicked shriek as he scooped up his Glock. Then he grabbed Holly and pulled her out of the way as the two vehicles roared past.

"Let me go!" Holly yanked her arm away from Stone's grip. She ran over to her Jeep Gladiator and climbed in. Meanwhile, Drummond dropped to one knee, picked up Scooby's fallen pistol, and sent three rounds after Darius' Lotus. One of the taillights exploded but the sports car sped off into the night.

"Damn that jackrabbit son of a bitch!" Drummond snarled. He stood up, walked over to Scooby, and kicked him in the crotch as hard as he could. The junkie cupped his hammered manhood, spewed vomit, and curled into the fetal position as Holly raced by in pursuit of Yvonne and Lizzy.

"Stay with Scooby and make sure his ass gets to jail," Stone said to Drummond. "I'm going after them."

He bolted for the Blazer, hit the gas, and went tearing out of the parking lot.

Up ahead, he saw muzzle flashes strobing the darkness and the sound of gunfire reached him even over the heavy growl of the truck's engine.

He spotted the taillights of Yvonne's SUV and the now-singular taillight of the Lotus as they reached the main road and took off like the hounds of hell were snapping at their heels.

He came up on the wreckage of Valentine's cruiser. Steam hissed from the hood and grill where the bullets had torn through. The windshield was a shattered mess of spider-webbed glass.

Stone barreled out of his Blazer and ran toward the shot-up patrol car. "Cade! You all right?"

He felt a flood of relief when Valentine sat up from where he'd been lying across the driver and passenger seats, out of the line of fire. Other than being covered in chunks of safety glass, the young deputy looked none the worse for wear. He gave Stone a thumbs up to signal his alive-and-well status.

Stone jumped back into his truck and took off after Darius and Yvonne. He had no intention of letting Holly face them alone.

———

"Drummond calling Sheriff Stone. You there? Over."

Stone grabbed the mic with his right hand and drove with his left, foot stomping hard on the gas. He prayed to God a deer didn't jump out in front of him because the results wouldn't be pretty, for the deer or the truck. "Stone here. Go ahead."

"Scooby got away."

"What?" Stone gritted his teeth. *Dammit!* "How?"

"Not sure." Drummond's embarrassment was evident even over the radio. "I was helping Valentine and when we turned around, the skinny bastard was gone."

"Keep looking. He can't be far. And when you find him, put a bullet in his kneecap so he can't run again."

A long pause, then, "Uh, are you serious, sheriff?"

"Use your discretion. Stone out."

He slammed the mic back into its cradle with a frustrated curse and then hit his lights and siren. The banshee wail pierced the night. Stone knew that for many people, that sound signaled salvation and rescue. But he had spent enough years on the killing fields to know that sometimes the good guys got there too late.

TWENTY-EIGHT

STONE FELT the weight of the darkness, internal and external, and all the secrets and sins it concealed.

He needed to rescue Lizzy and would do whatever that task required, including things that even God would struggle to forgive. But he would rather damn his soul and save Lizzy than face eternal judgement not having given his all to get her back. Darius and Yvonne would die when he caught up to them. For what they had done, they deserved to suck sulfur, not oxygen.

Stone thought of the charred corpse of Luisa Valdez, thought of the agony she must have endured at the end of her young life, and experienced a rush of white-hot rage.

No way was he letting that happen to Lizzy.

No way in hell.

———

Stone drove fast, using his familiarity with the roads and his tactical driving skills to push the Blazer right up to the edge of its limits. In the distance, whenever the road straightened, he could see taillights glowing in the darkness as Holly continued her pursuit of the Lotus and SUV.

Up ahead, Route 3 curved around a bend and the taillights momentarily vanished from Stone's line of sight. He nudged a little extra speed out of the already-screaming Blazer, eating up the asphalt. He knew he was pressing his luck but didn't want to lose them.

When he came out of the curve, he was staring at an empty road.

Where the hell did they go?

Route 3 stretched in front of him in a straight line for at least a mile. He should have been able to see their taillights. But there was nothing but blackness, the cold autumn night suffocating the landscape like an old scratchy blanket.

He whipped the Blazer over to the side of the road and called Holly on his cellphone.

She answered on the first ring. "Luke! Where are you?"

"I was right behind you but now I can't see your taillights."

"We turned onto North Waterford Road."

The Waterford office complex. Of course.

"On my way," he said and hung up. He twisted the wheel and gunned the Blazer back onto the road, loose gravel spitting out from under the tires in twin rooster tails.

He took the turn onto North Waterford Road recklessly hard, nearly rolling the truck. But he needed to catch up, fast, or Holly would be facing two very dangerous people alone.

He didn't remember North Waterford Road being this long. Potholes cratered the pavement and rusted guardrails bracketed both sides. Just another abandoned road scarring the beauty of the Adirondack region.

The complex appeared up ahead. The gate hung open. Stone raced through. Three vehicles—the Lotus, SUV, and Holly's Jeep—were arrayed haphazardly in front of the office building. Holly's was still running, the door open. Clearly she had bailed out in a hurry.

Stone exited the Blazer and kept low, wary of a bullet-happy welcoming party. But none materialized.

Something drew his attention, causing him to glance up. Behind one of the second floor windows, a firefly-quick flash of illumination, like someone turning a flashlight on and off as quick as possible.

Stone reached in and switched off Holly's vehicle. With the engine no longer running, a deep silence fell over the complex. It was so quiet, Stone felt like he could almost hear the sizzle of the stars scattered across the clear night sky.

He moved away from Holly's Jeep Gladiator into the deepest shadows he could find. With his Glock drawn, he held his breath and listened, attuning his senses to the darkness.

Not a trace of sound anywhere in the vicinity.

That meant they were all inside. Stone scanned the main building in front of him. His gut told him the flashlight he had spotted on the second floor was a decoy, bait meant to draw him into a trap. Darius was probably lurking near the entrance, waiting to spring an ambush, maybe even a good old-fashioned back-shooting.

Stone evaluated his position. The shadows in which he stood were clutched within a grove of decorative bushes, part of the corporate landscaping that had somehow survived a decade of abandonment. A low cement planter enclosed the landscaping area fronting the entrance. Stone crouched down and followed it to the edge of the bushes, then peered around the edge to study the building's entryway.

After a few moments, a shadow shifted within the glass vestibule.

Darius. Had to be. Stone seriously doubted Yvonne would hang back to do the bushwhacking herself. No, she would let her minion get his hands dirty. Darius enjoyed killing, so it made sense that he would be the one lurking in the dark to take Stone out.

Stone cursed under his breath. If they had set a trap for him, it meant they probably had Holly now, too.

He slid deeper into the shadows, searching for an alternate entrance.

———

But they didn't have Holly.

Not yet anyway.

She was inside the building, hunkered down by the stairwell in the lobby where she'd hastily hidden when Darius appeared and posted up in the vestibule, presumably to ambush Stone.

She had known danger before. Hell, she was in the WITSEC program because she had run away from her vicious mob boss husband. And less than a year ago she had confronted and killed a murderous survivalist who broke into her home and threatened them. Yeah, she knew all too well what it felt like to be hunted.

Now it was her turn to do the hunting.

She felt something dark and dangerous burning inside her, a deep, primal impulse that flooded her veins with enraged energy. Her senses quickened. She felt attuned to the sights, sounds, and scents around her. She inhaled long and slow, drawing in a deep breath.

She smelled the decaying musk of mold, the earthiness of worn wood, the sharp bite of Darius' aftershave. And just beneath it all, like a secret layer, the faintest hint of Lizzy's perfume. Her daughter had passed this way, up the stairwell, not long ago.

She glanced back over at Darius. She had no gun, no way to take him out, as he laid in wait. She cared for Stone in ways that her heart was not ready to fully admit, but Lizzy was her priority right now. She would just have to trust Stone to take care of himself.

She slipped off her shoes. Keeping an eye on Darius to make sure his back remained turned, she crept around to the front of the stairs and ghosted up them, silent on bare feet, heading for the second floor.

―――

Stone found his access point around back on the ground floor.

After the software company pulled up stakes and departed the Waterford office complex, the place had become a popular hangout spot for teens from Plattsburgh and Milton. They scaled the fence, drank beer, tagged the buildings with graffiti, and smashed out windows.

Stone found a plate-glass panel someone had punched a jagged hole through. It resembled a mouth filled with sharp fangs. He peered inside and saw a breakroom, complete with a kitchenette and a half-dozen circular lunch tables. On the tiled floor, surrounded by a spray of broken glass, lay the large rock someone had heaved through the window.

The hole was not big enough for a man to get through. Stone aimed a boot heel at the bottom of the aperture and kicked out more glass until he was able to duck into the room. He was far enough away from the front entrance that he seriously doubted Darius heard the sound of glass breaking, but he didn't know where Yvonne and Lizzy were.

He stepped into the corner of the room, aimed his Glock at the door, and waited. He mentally counted off two minutes, listening, ready for violence if anyone had heard him break in and came looking.

No one came.

He left the breakroom, eased into the hallway, and headed toward the lobby.

———

Holly reached the top of the stairs, her brain churning with alarmist thoughts.

Yvonne is armed. She has Lizzy. I'm outmatched.

She cursed herself for not grabbing her Springfield XDS 9mm pistol when she left her house with Stone that afternoon. She hadn't been thinking clearly when he broke the news to her that Lizzy had been kidnapped. All she had was the silver cross around her neck that concealed a small dagger.

Well, she might not have a gun, but she had plenty of maternal fury. The primal feeling stirred within her, a rising tide of rage that blotted out stumbling blocks like fear and hesitation.

Lizzy was in danger. Saving her was the only thing that mattered.

Right now, Holly felt more feral than human, an unfamiliar, intoxicating state of being. Energy buzzed in her brain, setting her synapses ablaze, the fire pulsing through her veins. She felt attuned to her surroundings, alive, focused, and utterly devoid of fear.

She closed her eyes, listening to the dark, letting her gut instinct tell her where to go.

Where are you, Lizzy?

She felt an almost telepathic pull tugging her forward.

Silently, she moved deeper into the shadows.

———

Stone reached an interior entrance that opened into the main lobby and cautiously peered around the edge. He saw a stairwell rising to the second floor and overturned reception area furniture scattered about. His eyes shifted to the glass vestibule where Darius had been lying in wait for him.

It was empty

Stone crept forward. He noticed the front door was open. Darius stood outside, talking to someone. Stone shifted position to get a better angle and recognized Scooby, standing next to a car that he had undoubtedly stolen. Looked like the little weasel had run right back to his masters after giving Drummond the slip.

Stone took advantage of their distraction to cross the lobby to the stairs. His boot connected with something on the ground and he looked down.

Holly's shoes.

Stone recognized what she had done. Slipped off her shoes to hunt her prey barefoot like some kind of primitive, prehistoric tribeswoman.

Nothing was more dangerous than getting between a mama bear and her cub, Stone thought. Yvonne Brossard had no idea what kind of rage she had unleashed within Holly.

He ghosted up the stairs, looking for a target. Because even kill-crazy mama bears needed backup sometimes.

TWENTY-NINE

LIZZY? *Honey? Where are you?*

Holly formed the question over and over again in her mind, remembering the early days of Lizzy's infancy, when she and her daughter had shared the magical connection that exists between mother and child. The teenage years may have strained that bond but it remained unbroken.

Holly hid in the shadows of an office doorway on the second floor. Her senses felt heightened—sharpened eyesight and smell, and tactile sensations in her hands and feet. Nature, giving her the edge she needed to fulfill her role as mother and protector.

Traditionally, men defended the tribe and family. But what happened when the men fell? It became time for the women to rise up as warriors.

A weird madness stirred in Holly's blood, a strange sense of being connected to everything on a molecular level. She had felt the same way when Lizzy was just a baby, all big eyes and tiny fingers, clinging to Holly for dear life. She had felt needed, an innocent life depending on her, trusting her to have the strength to the do the impossible and unthinkable if that's what was called for.

Like now.

She inched ahead into the darkness. She moved like a lioness, guided by instinct, by the feel of the terrain under her feet, by the razor-sharp awareness of every shape and shadow ahead. Her lips peeled back from her teeth like a she-wolf baring her fangs. She clenched and unclenched her fists, fingers curving like claws. Her nails weren't long, but they were long enough to sink through flesh and tear out Yvonne Brossard's trachea if given the opportunity.

Whatever it takes, she thought. *That's what I'm willing to do.*

Losing Lizzy would be like a dagger to the heart, a wound from which she would never recover. She could not allow it. *Would not* allow it.

She heard movement somewhere on the darkened floor ahead. She crouched low and crept forward, keeping to the shadows.

———

When Stone reached the top of the stairs, he caught movement from the corner of his eye. Turning his head, he saw that Darius and Scooby had parted company. Yvonne's henchman returned to his position in the glass vestibule while the junkie climbed into the SUV. Their actions gave no indication as to what they had talked about. The SUV's headlights blazed open the darkness as Scooby went tearing down the road, heading back toward Route 3. Going for reinforcements? Running for the border? Stone had no idea and he let it go for now. There'd be time enough to deal with Scooby later, after Lizzy and Holly were safe.

Down in the vestibule, Darius pulled out a cellphone. Stone watched silently as he quickly sent a text.

Somewhere in the depths of the second floor, Stone heard a distant, electronic chime as someone received the message.

Yvonne.

She hadn't silenced her phone. A mistake. One that Stone hoped she wouldn't live long enough to regret.

He headed in the direction of the sound.

———

Lizzy, her hands zip-tied behind her, stumbled along the darkened hallway, feet scuffing on the carpet. Yvonne's fingers dug viciously into the flesh of her bicep. The Canadian woman was taller and stronger, forcing Lizzy deeper into the office complex, her violent grip threatening even more pain.

They reached a landing. A hexagonal section of floor, ringed by glassed-in guardrails, provided a view of a lobby fountain on the lower level.

Yvonne jerked her to a halt with such force that she nearly ripped Lizzy's arm out of its socket. Lizzy heard a cellphone chime and watched Yvonne haul hers out of a pocket, quickly switch it to silent mode, and then check the text message.

"You need to let me go," Lizzy said. "You have no idea what you've gotten yourself into."

Yvonne hit her. Not a casual slap, but a closed fist to the mouth that smashed Lizzy's teeth against her lips and left them bloodied. Then her hand was in Lizzy's hair, fingernails tearing ruts from her scalp, jerking her head back.

"Do you know what it's like to spend your life building a dream?" Yvonne snarled with her face inches from Lizzy's. "I came up from nothing. *Nothing.* My mother worked in a factory while my father did nothing but get drunk all the time. I built my business one customer, one sale, one alliance at a time. You think you can threaten me? You're the one in danger, you little bitch. Bet on it."

"You'll find out who's in danger when my mother or Stone catches up to you," Lizzy retorted. "Bet on *that*."

Yvonne lined up to hit her a second time, but Lizzy was ready. Before the fist flew, Lizzy spat directly into Yvonne's face. Her eyes closed reflexively and Lizzy shoulder-checked her against the wall and fled down the nearest hallway.

———

Holly heard the soft chime of a text arriving. It was somewhere close by. She held her breath and angled toward it, moving like a jungle cat closing in for the kill.

———

Lizzy ran blindly. The way her hands were bound behind her made it difficult to turn and look, but she knew Yvonne was somewhere behind her and likely gaining ground fast. Lizzy knew the woman would take revenge and that it would be painful. The knowledge poured power into her legs. She ran desperately, looking for a place to hide and find something to cut these straps from her wrists.

But where?

Her legs churned. She saw nowhere that offered safety and concealment. The breath tore from her throat in quick, ragged gasps. She rounded a corner, flattened herself against the wall, and fired off a desperate prayer.

She heard the sound of running footsteps approaching. Yvonne was getting close.

Lizzy looked frantically left and right. Then her eyes focused on what was directly across the hall from her.

An EXIT sign hung above a steel fire door equipped with a crash bar.

She came off the wall, darted over to the door, and pushed it open. She found herself on a fire escape, metal stairs bolted to the side of the building.

Which way should I go? Up or down?

Her thoughts raced desperately.

Last she knew, Darius was skulking around the ground level. She didn't want to escape Yvonne's clutches only to run into the henchman's arms. Plus, Stone had once told her to always take the high ground if it was available.

She began to climb, heading for the roof.

———

Stone heard a fire door crash open and then slam shut somewhere in the building. It sounded like it came from one of the upper floors.

He ran up the stairs two at a time, still staying as silent as possible.

———

Holly ran toward the metallic noise of the fire door opening and banging shut. It was close, very close.

She moved through the dark, hunting for an EXIT sign. She found one quickly and pushed open the door to hear footsteps pounding on the metal-grate steps above her.

"Lizzy?"

And then Yvonne tackled her from behind. The two women spilled onto the small landing.

———

"Mom?"

Lizzy turned around at the sound of her mother's voice and started back down the stairs.

———

Holly heard Yvonne grunt as she went down, knees and elbows banging off metal. Yvonne's pistol skittered away.

Holly recovered quickly, pushing with her hands to rise up on all fours. She spotted the dark shape of the pistol near the edge of the steps.

She and Yvonne dove for the gun at the same time. Their hands collided, fingers scrambling for purchase. The pistol was knocked away, sliding over the edge and tumbling down the stairs into the darkness below.

Holly rolled onto her side and lashed out with her right hand, hitting Yvonne in the face. The blow rocked Yvonne's head to the side.

From above, Holly heard Lizzy's voice.

"Mom?"

"Lizzy!" Holly lunged toward the stairs leading to the building's upper levels. But Yvonne moved quicker than expected, pouncing on her like a cat attacking a mouse.

Holly felt the weight and strength of the Canadian woman crash against her. She fell forward against the steps, the metal edge digging into her ribs hard enough to make her gasp. She managed to swing around and face Yvonne, both of them on their knees, hands in each other's hair, ripping and tearing.

Holly was running on pure fighting instinct right

now, energy burning through her veins like molten steel. She let go of Yvonne's hair long enough to punch the bitch in the face again. The blow struck with a satisfying smack. Yvonne recoiled with a cry of shock and pain.

Holly reached for her, curved fingers clawing for eyes, hair, throat—whatever she could get her hands on. Despite the cold night air, she felt sweat baptizing her body, making her clothes stick to her skin. Her hands narrowly missed grabbing Yvonne's hair and scalping her by the roots.

A blow to the side of her head sent her reeling. Holly raised her arms to ward off another strike. Yvonne pressed forward with vicious elbow sweeps that battered down Holly's defenses. Her fingers speared toward Holly's throat, forcing her back.

"Mom?"

Lizzy appeared on the landing above.

"Lizzy!" Holly reached for the railing and pulled herself up to her feet.

Yvonne leaned back and kicked out as hard as she could.

Holly screamed as the blow impacted against the side of her knee. The leg buckled and she fell down, still grasping the railing. She let go and rolled away, toward the steps leading downward.

Yvonne smiled triumphantly and kicked out again, her foot smashing into Holly's already bruised ribcage.

Holly tumbled down the stairs and crashed hard on the grate-metal landing below. Her head banged painfully off one of the steps and a blackness that had nothing to do with the night rushed through her brain.

The last thing she saw was Yvonne grabbing Lizzy's arm and forcing her back through the fire door. The last thing she heard was her daughter's anguished cry.

THIRTY

STONE HEARD a fire door open and shut again on the floor above him. He retreated to the stairway, moving ghost-silent just like he'd been trained during his warrior days. Using the rail for leverage, he ascended the steps two at a time. At the top, he found himself in a long hallway.

Gun up and at the ready, he eased down the corridor. He listened but couldn't hear anything. No sound to betray the presence of the targets he sought. He fired off another prayer for Lizzy's safety, followed by one asking God to give him the chance to put a bullet in Yvonne Brossard's black heart. Because even God despised people who hurt kids.

The silence was broken by voices up ahead. Muffled talking, followed by a sharp cry of pain. Stone recognized Lizzy's voice, even with the suffering edge laced onto it. The evil cackle that followed was Yvonne's, clearly amused by the hurt she was causing.

Stone experienced a fresh burst of rage. These psychopaths seemed to get off on hurting kids. He had seen this brand of sadism in some of the men he had hunted during his warrior days, but rarely had he stumbled across it in a woman.

Yvonne was a sick bitch.

Stone followed the voices into the darkness.

This, the third floor, appeared to be the aerie of the elites back in the days of the software company. The carpet was richer than the utilitarian flooring found elsewhere in the building, the walls paneled with mahogany. Even after years of idleness, neglect, and vandalism, the upscale décor was obvious. Even the floor layout was different, with executive suites situated around a set of cubicles where once upon a time secretaries and personal assistants had slaved for their corporate overlords.

Stone heard the voices again, followed by a crashing noise and then the sound of casters on an office chair being moved into position.

Ducking low behind some portable half-wall partitions, he moved closer. Adrenaline pulsed through his system but he kept it under control. It would fuel his actions when the moment came, but he would not let it be his master.

He tightened his grip on the Glock as he peered into the shadows. Lizzy's voice floated out of the darkness to him.

"Let me go or else—"

A slap cut off her words. Stone heard the crack of flesh hitting flesh, heard the gasp of pain from Lizzy.

"Or else what?" Yvonne snarled. "Who do you think holds the cards here, huh? Your mother is a sack of broken bones where I kicked her down the stairs and by now Darius has taken out the cowboy sheriff you think is going to ride in on a white horse and rescue your ass. Newsflash, little girl—nobody is coming for you. Nobody."

You're dead wrong, Stone thought. *Somebody is coming for her all right.*

He took a deep breath and exhaled slowly. It was do or die time. The gun felt good in his fist, ready to deal out hollow-point justice.

"Time for you to be reunited with your girlfriend," Yvonne said. "You'll be able to talk about how you both died the exact same way."

"What are you doing?" Lizzy's voice sounded panicked. Stone heard a liquid splashing noise, followed by the rasp of a lighter being fired up. "No, please...not like this. Not like this!"

Stone rose from his crouch and stepped into view. He saw Lizzy zip-tied to an office chair near a glassed-in guard rail that offered a split-level view of the floor below. Her hair was wet and plastered to her head and he could smell the lighter fluid even from ten meters away.

Yvonne turned, silhouetted against the shiny chrome of the elevator doors behind her. She wore a cold grin on her face and a lit cigarette dangled from her left-hand fingertips, hovering over Lizzy's soaked head. If Stone shot her now, the cigarette would fall and set Lizzy ablaze.

He kept his finger tight on the trigger but knew he would have to wait.

"Well, look who showed up to the rodeo." Yvonne brandished the can of lighter fluid in her right hand. "I assume Darius is dead?"

"Not yet," Stone said. "I'll get to him next. I wanted to kill the queen bitch first."

A line of ash hung from the burning cigarette. "How do you like your teenager, cowboy?" Yvonne asked. "Medium rare or extra crispy?"

"If she burns, so do you."

Yvonne ignored the threat and said, "Drop the gun."

Stone didn't waste time resisting. With the cigarette looming like a guillotine over Lizzy's flammable head, he couldn't risk a shot anyway. He let the Glock fall to the floor and held his hands away from his body in a nonthreatening manner.

"Good," Yvonne said. "Now I want you to—"

The elevator chimed.

Yvonne stopped talking and turned her head as the doors opened.

The elevator car was empty.

"What the hell?" She turned back toward Stone. "What kind of game are you playing?"

Stone said nothing as a shape dropped down from the escape hatch in the elevator, landing silently on bare feet and stepping out as the doors closed behind her. He kept his eyes locked on Yvonne, not wanting to glance at Holly and betray her presence.

She emerged from the shadows like a vengeful ghost, stalking her nemesis from behind.

Yvonne was caught completely by surprise as Holly's clawed hand reached around and ripped the right side of her face. Her other hand lashed out and knocked the cigarette away. It landed on the carpet, mere inches from the edge of the pool of lighter fluid in which Lizzy sat.

Yvonne howled in shock and pain and twisted away. She kicked out at Holly but Stone didn't see if she connected. By then, he was moving as fast as he could toward Lizzy.

He reached the chair she was strapped to and quickly kicked away the smoldering cigarette. It tumbled across the carpet, sprinkling ash in its wake.

The two woman circled each other, Holly's hands raised to chest level, fingers curled into claws, while Yvonne adopted a more classic fighter stance that evidenced some martial arts training. Yvonne lunged forward and launched a tentative strike, testing her opponent's defenses. Holly backed away, her angry eyes locked on Yvonne with unblinking intent.

Stone grabbed the back of Lizzy's chair and pulled her out of harm's way, rolling her behind a nearby desk. Satisfied she was momentarily safe, he went back for his gun.

The two women grappled together. Holly's arms encircled Yvonne's waist, trying to squeeze the life out of her. Yvonne's left hand was wrapped in Holly's hair while her right landed punishing body blows.

"Stupid bitch! I'll kill you!" Yvonne punctuated every word with a savage punch.

Holly grunted in pain, her resolve flagging beneath the brutal assault. But somehow she found the strength to hang on.

Stone grabbed up his pistol and pivoted on his heel, turning toward the two combatants. The Glock swung into firing position, the gunsights seeking target acquisition.

Yvonne reared back, her hand bladed to strike the back of Holly's neck. Stone knew that if the blow landed, it could sever the spinal cord and kill her.

No chance in hell was he letting that happen.

But before he could get off a shot, Holly let out a primal scream and pushed with all her strength. Yvonne stumbled backward, collided with a desk, and overbalanced. She landed flat on her back, Holly looming over her.

Stone edged sideways, toward the center of the room. Holly now blocked his shot, so he needed a new angle to put a bullet in Yvonne.

Turned out, it wasn't necessary.

"You *bitch!*" Holly spat. She grabbed the bottom of the

silver cross hanging from her neck and pulled down to release the hidden dagger.

Then she stabbed it into Yvonne's left eye.

The small blade wasn't long enough to punch through the back of the socket and penetrate the brain, but it was more than long enough to make the eyeball burst apart in a bloody mess.

"You bitch!" Holly screamed again. "You hurt my baby girl!"

Yvonne howled in pain. It had no effect on Holly. She ripped the knife out and drove it into Yvonne's other eye. Completely blinded, Yvonne thrashed on the desktop like a salted slug, fingers clutching at her savaged sockets.

Holly grabbed her by the hair and dragged her off the desk and toward the edge of the balcony overlooking the lower level. Holly looked like she had gone mad and Stone couldn't blame her one bit. Mess with the kid, you mess with the mother.

Holly hauled Yvonne over to the balcony's rail—"Rot in hell, you bitch!"—and shoved her over.

Yvonne plummeted two stories, screaming the whole way down, until she landed headfirst on the marble floor below. Stone heard the sickening crunch of her skull shattering on impact.

THIRTY-ONE

"LIZZY!"

Holly ran over to her daughter and fell on her knees beside the office chair. Lizzy, soaked in lighter fluid and more scared than she probably wanted to admit, wept as Stone cut through the zip-ties.

"It's okay, Lizzy. I'm here, sweetheart, I'm here." Holly folded her arms around her daughter and cried right along with her.

From outside, Stone heard the rumbling roar of an engine racing through the night. He ran over to the windows that faced the main entrance and saw the Lotus speeding down the access road. Looked like Darius had decided to make a getaway attempt rather than stick around to avenge his boss's death.

"Stay here," Stone said, heading for the stairs. "I'm going after that son of a bitch."

Holly nodded as she continued to hold her daughter like she would never let go of her again.

―――――

The Lotus' taillight—the one not shot out back at the high-school—was a tiny pinprick receding into the darkness by the time Stone raced out the front door. He jumped into the Blazer, hit the ignition, and tore off in hot pursuit.

Ordinarily, the Lotus would outpace the Blazer by a significant margin. But Darius didn't know these back roads as well as Stone and couldn't push the sports car to its limits. The Blazer steadily closed the gap.

Making conditions worse, a cold rain had started to drizzle down, slickening the asphalt. Stone saw the Lotus' rear end skew sideways going around a sharp bend, the spinning wheels momentarily losing their grip on the wet road. Darius recovered but sacrificed some speed in the process. Stone surged ahead, gaining more ground, coming up hot on the Lotus' tail.

Jaw clenched, face grim, he tried to coax even more speed from the Blazer so he could ram Darius right off the road. If the bastard was lucky, he would perish in the fiery crash. Because what Stone had planned for him was worse. His rage was a nuclear fire in his veins, scorching away all thoughts except those that involved raw, lethal justice.

In the all-consuming heat of this moment, he wasn't a cop or a preacher. He was just a hard, uncompromising man determined to exterminate evil no matter the cost. There would be time enough later to mull over the moral and spiritual implications of the killing. Right now, all that mattered was getting the job done.

The hunt was on. Somebody was dying tonight.

He just hoped it wouldn't be him.

The road straightened and the Lotus poured on the speed, widening the gap between the two vehicles. Stone white-knuckled the Blazer's steering wheel and kept the gas pedal pinned to the floor. The tires devoured the road as they tore through the night. Raindrops splattered against the windshield like liquid bullets and were whisked away by the wipers.

He didn't call for backup because he didn't *want* backup. For what he planned to do to Darius, witnesses would be a problem. Some deeds were best done alone, in secret.

The Lotus took a sharp left turn, skidding sideways on the wet pavement until the wheels found traction again. The car gunned forward onto a narrow dirt road, not much wider than a tractor lane.

Stone took the turn as well, trying to recall where the road went. If memory served, it wound east through an old farmstead before bearing north toward the border. Darius was either trying to shake him off or trying to avoid a high-speed chase into downtown Plattsburgh, which is where the main road would have taken them.

The rain intensified. The droplets came down harder, silver bombs that hammered the Blazer. The Lotus' tail-light was nothing more than a red smudge in the wet, soaking darkness.

The road abruptly forked. The Lotus jerked to the right, sloughing past a rickety windmill that thrust up into the night like a decrepit shadow. Stone glimpsed the large, half-rotten paddles as he sped past, gaining lost ground. The structure reminded him of some ancient, alien monstrosity.

In the headlights, Stone saw the fence lining the sides of the dirt track. Strands of rusted barbed wire drooped between the wooden posts, doing a piss-poor job of protecting the barren fields.

The two vehicles barreled into the abandoned barn-yard, mud spraying up from their tires. As the Lotus maneuvered to the left, Stone managed to clip the rear end of the sports car with the heavy-duty brush guard mounted on the front of the Blazer.

The Lotus spun sideways and crashed passenger side first into some kind of farm equipment with a spiked roller—an agricultural aerator. The rusted spikes impaled the sleek bodywork and punctured the tires, rendering the car immobile.

As Stone slammed his brakes, he saw the driver-side window going down. Darius' arm emerged, holding a gun. The muzzle flash looked like lightning in the rain.

Glass exploded all over Stone.

THIRTY-TWO

STONE INSTINCTIVELY DUCKED down as the window blew apart and sprayed glass all over him. He felt the thudding vibration of the bullet burying itself in the headrest. A damn close call, but this wasn't the first time he'd felt the Reaper's cold, graveyard breath on the back of his neck.

He stayed hunkered down as two more quick shots rang out. They punched into the frame of the truck but neither came as close as the first.

When he sat up, he saw the Lotus' driver-side door hanging open. The dome light revealed the car was empty. He glimpsed the shadow-shape of Darius running toward a nearby barn.

Stone cranked the steering wheel and gunned the gas, whipping the Blazer around so that the headlights pinned Darius in their harsh glare. The truck surged forward as if hungry for the kill, bumping and banging over the ruts in the barnyard like a bucking bronco.

As Stone closed on Darius, the henchman twisted around and fired again. The first shot starred the windshield and whistled past Stone's head; the second bullet took out one of the front tires.

The Blazer slowed as the flattened tire sank into the mud. Snarling a curse, Stone brought the truck to a halt, flung open the door, and launched himself into the night. The rain pelted against his Stetson, running off the brim in rivulets.

Up head, Darius ran out of range of the headlights. But his forward trajectory indicated he was still heading for the barn. Stone grabbed a tactical flashlight from the Blazer's glovebox and lit out after him with his Glock drawn.

The wet ground sucked at his boots as he ran. He could just make out a shadowy glimpse of Darius ducking into the barn, the large building looming in the darkness ahead.

Maybe there's an old pitchfork in there I can stab him with, Stone thought. He was sometimes surprised how easily he slipped into his old warrior ways. When the time came, killing came easy.

No backup. No reinforcements. Nobody covering his six.

Just the way Stone wanted it.

He plunged into the shadows of the barn.

He paused inside, listening to the darkness. This far from the city and with the moon shrouded in rainclouds, there was almost no ambient light to work with. He didn't turn on his flashlight because it would just make him a target, give Darius a point of reference to shoot at.

He heard footsteps somewhere in the depths of the barn. The sound of someone breathing. Then nothing but silence. Darius had holed up somewhere inside.

Stone knew he should call for additional units, but the hell with that. One on one, man to man…that's how this was going to play out. There might be a badge pinned to his coat but this wasn't about the law, it was about justice. That was just the way he was built.

Darius was an evil son of a bitch. A monster who had burned a teenage girl alive for no other reason than to "send a message" to her father. Stone intended to punch him a one-way ticket straight to hell.

Stone edged along the wall, moving cautiously in the darkness. The temptation to use his flashlight was strong but he ignored it. He was trained to operate in the dark.

The barn smelled like hay and dung, reminding him of summers in Texas. The air was dry and stale despite the rain coming down outside and dripping through cracks in the roof. The scent of livestock still lingered despite how many years the farmstead had been abandoned.

Wherever Darius was hiding, he was being very quiet. Stone's combat instincts detected the man's presence but couldn't pinpoint his location. Moonlight would have helped, laced the shadows with some silver, but the rain-clouds throttled the sky and left everything black.

Stone was trained to use his other senses when he couldn't see, when his vision had been compromised. If Darius thought the blackness would save him, he was very, very wrong. Soldiers had been fighting in the dark since wars were created. Hell, the tunnel rats in Vietnam had practically made an art form out of it. What was a major drawback for Darius was nothing more than a minor inconvenience for Stone.

Time to maximize his advantage.

He felt his other senses heighten. The dry, woody barnyard aroma continued to clog up his sinuses. He moved forward slowly, an inch at a time, probing the ground with his boots. He felt a plank under his foot and stepped over it carefully, not wanting to catch a nail in the heel.

He moved deeper into the barn, one hand holding the Glock, the other stretched out in front of him. His fingers touched up against a solid surface. Cautious exploration revealed he was standing next to some kind of stall. The lingering scent smelled of horses.

He melted further into the darkness, ears tuned for any sound that would hint at his enemy's position. Once, he thought he heard a muffled sneeze, but with the sound of the rain on the roof, he couldn't be sure.

Was that you, Darius? Probably wondering if I'm still coming for you. Don't worry, I'm still here. In the dark. Hunting.

Stone eased to the left, in the direction he thought the sound had originated. If he could get a fix on Darius' location, he would blind him with the flashlight and hopefully get off a kill-shot before the enforcer even knew what hit him.

But a moment later, he wasn't the one doing the shooting.

He had just taken another step forward when a gunshot boomed like thunder, the muzzle flash lighting up the darkness with a piercing tongue of orange fire. Stone caught a half-second glimpse of Darius firing blindly before the darkness engulfed them again.

Stone recognized the shot for what it was—panic fire. The tension of hiding in the pitch-black barn, not sure where or when Stone would appear, had frayed the man's nerves.

"Hey, cowboy!" Darius called out. "Let's stop playing hide 'n' seek and make a deal."

Stone kept his mouth shut. The sound of his voice would just give Darius a target.

Another gunshot rang out. Another wild shot in the dark. Stone heard the bullet sizzle past, missing by a wide margin. This time, in the half-second strobe of the muzzle flash, he saw a wooden ladder rising up to a hayloft, Darius standing at the base.

A moment later, as the darkness descended again, Stone heard the distinct sound of wood creaking. Darius was climbing the ladder.

Stone visualized the scene, his mind mapping out what his eyes could not see. He raised the Glock and fired into the dark. A shriek of pain from Darius let him know the bullet had struck flesh.

He fired again, angling the pistol upward to compensate for Darius climbing the ladder and was rewarded with another howl. Then came the dry sound of wood splintering, followed by a wetter crack that sounded like breaking bone. Darius' shrieks and howls turned into full-fledged screams.

Stone activated his flashlight. He located the bottom of the ladder and spotted Darius' gun lying on the barn floor, blood droplets spattered around it. Stone panned upwards until he found Darius himself.

At some point while climbing the ladder, one of the rungs had broken under the henchman's foot, trapping it. Entangled, he had fallen backward at an odd angle, all his weight causing his leg to break and leaving him hanging upside down.

Darius twisted back and forth, face contorted in pain as his snapped shinbone bulged grotesquely beneath the surface of the skin, threatening to tear through. His hands scrabbled to reach the ladder but his efforts were in vain, the angle all wrong. Blood dripped from a bullet hole in his shoulder and another one in his left flank, evidence of Stone's shot-in-the-dark marksmanship.

Stone walked over and kicked away the fallen gun. Habit, more than anything, since it wasn't like Darius could reach the weapon while he dangled upside down with a broken leg.

"Looks like you're kind of in a tough spot," Stone said.

"Help me." Darius teeth were gritted in pain, eyes squeezed shut against the harsh glare of the flashlight. "My fucking leg…get me down from here."

"Yeah, I noticed your leg is all messed up."

Stone swung the flashlight to the left and saw a workbench fastened to the wall. An old oil lantern hung from a rusted nail nearby and there was a container of liquid kerosene on an upper shelf. Stone walked over and shook it. Half full, maybe a little more. He found a box of matches on the bench, half-buried beneath some old horseshoes.

He filled the lantern and lit it with a match. He turned off the flashlight, put it back in his pocket, and carried the lantern over and set it down at the foot of the ladder. The warm glow seemed almost cozy despite the dripping blood and the cursing man hanging upside down from a broken leg.

"Fuck me, it hurts," Darius groaned. "Get me down."

"Don't worry, it won't hurt much longer," Stone said. "But first, a question. The Valdez family. You and Yvonne were using them?"

"Yes. Yes! Fuck, yes!" Darius shouted, as if the sheer volume of his confession would somehow force back the pain. "My leg…feels like it's…"

"Tearing apart?" Stone said. "That's because you've got a compound fracture and your shinbone is ripping through your skin."

"Get me down." Darius looked like he was on the verge of unconsciousness. "My leg's going to come off."

"Doesn't work like that," Stone said. "Human tendons are a lot stronger than people realize. You could hang by a tendon for days. Yeah, it'd hurt like a son of a bitch, but you could do it."

Darius closed his eyes, mouth making mewling sounds as a horrified sob tremored his body.

"When Valdez didn't play ball, you decided to send a message and burned their daughter alive."

It wasn't a question but Darius nodded anyway, as if acknowledging his sin would save him. His face had turned bright red from all the blood rushing to his head, making him look like a blister ready to pop.

"Now it's my turn to send a message." Stone grabbed the kerosene off the bench and poured half the bottle on the ground. The strong, heady fumes assaulted his nostrils as the flammable liquid spread in a puddle at the base of the wooden ladder.

Darius watched, eyes wide and terrified.

Stone splashed the rest of the kerosene all over the henchman's trapped body, soaking his clothes. Darius sputtered as the foul liquid streamed down his face.

"Eye for an eye, tooth for tooth, flame for flame," Stone said. "Some might call it revenge. But not me."

Stone tossed aside the empty container and struck a match.

"No," he continued, "I call it justice. Justice for a little girl." The match flickered, blackening the wooden stick as it burned down toward his fingers. "Any last words?"

Darius screamed. A raw, inarticulate cry of terror. It came from deep inside him, spilling from his lungs and over his lips. But it did nothing to sway Stone's cold determination.

The match burned lower. He could feel the heat on his fingertips. "I want you to think about her, Darius. Think about the little girl you burned alive. Remember her face, because where you're going, you won't be seeing her."

Darius thrashed as horror, despair, and desolation darkened his eyes. He looked at Stone's implacable face and saw his own ending.

"Burn in hell, you son of a bitch," Stone rasped, and tossed the match.

The kerosene ignited with an explosive whoosh. Fire immediately flared up and engulfed Darius' body. He opened his mouth to scream and the flames scorched down his throat, burning, blistering, blackening.

Stone watched until the flesh started to melt off the henchman's skull, then turned and walked out of the barn. The fire spread across the floor and crawled up the ladder to the hay loft. It wouldn't take long for the old building to burn to the ground, a backroad funeral pyre for a child killer.

The tormented cries coming from Darius' charred esophagus were horrible, but Stone felt no pity. His sense of justice was raw and primal and sometimes ugly…but it was still justice.

Outside, the cold rain continued to fall. Stone stood, alone with God and his thoughts, and watched the blaze suffuse the night with its orange, flickering glow. The inferno started to roar like an angry, living beast. The roof over the hay loft collapsed and sent sparks swirling into the night.

Despite the crackling roar and raging intensity of the flames, Darius continued to scream from inside the hellish depths of the inferno.

But not for long.

THIRTY-THREE

THE NEXT DAY, Stone received a call from Captain Chandler.

"We've arrested half a dozen people involved with Yvonne Brossard's criminal enterprise," Chandler informed him. "Turns out the roots run deep. They're even connected to our nightclub shooting. Needless to say, we've got a lot of investigative work ahead of us."

Stone leaned back in his office chair. "Did you go through the car Yvonne wanted back so badly?"

"Sure did," Chandler replied. "There was enough crystal meth packed into the sideboards to sink a battleship."

"So she was running a smuggling operation."

"It was more sophisticated than that," said Chandler. "From what we've gathered, it looks like Brossard and Darius coordinated the operations of literally dozens of small-time meth cooks. They had a web of suppliers reaching as far as Manitoba, if you can believe it. The Crown prosecutor is churning out warrants like handbills."

"So Yvonne and Darius were at the top of a pyramid of suppliers."

"More like the center of a web." Stone heard the sound of papers shuffling, presumably Chandler checking his notes. "The operation had serious legs and she was looking to expand overseas, believe it or not. The setup was brilliant in its simplicity. Think about it—what does every meth-head want?"

"More meth?"

"Right, more meth. Specifically, they want money to buy meth. Better yet, they want to be able to make it themselves and create their own high. Being the clever scumbags they are—or *were*, rather—Brossard and Darius took advantage of both these impulses. They identified small-time users who were willing to set up as cooks and offered them seed money."

"Sort of a bad Samaritan for meth-heads," Stone said, realizing that's how Scooby and Dale had pulled it off.

"Small investment, really, when you think about it," Chandler continued. "Some chemicals, enough money to rent workspace like a house or apartment."

"Or a trailer or storage unit," Stone added.

"With Brossard supplying the money, the cooks were expected to produce. If they did, they were rewarded with more money and more meth. But it's an unstable arrangement, because at some point, the meth-head is going to start consuming his own product and cutting into the profit margins. Once they reach that point of no return-on-investment, Brossard would simply withdraw support and find someone else."

"Which created competition among suppliers," Stone said.

"Exactly."

"That explains all the damn fires I had around here." *Most of them, anyway,* he silently added. Somehow he doubted Cynthia Gunther's death had anything to do with a drug war. He had Valentine looking into that case while he was on the phone. "Couple of our local junkies got caught up in this bad Samaritan scheme. Yvonne recruited them both and they started burning each other's labs down to gain an advantage."

"At least now you can close the book on those cases."

"Got one fire that still doesn't make sense, but I'll figure it out." Stone glanced at the clock. Valentine should be bringing him a report soon. "But at least we have both parties locked up until we can figure out the details." Scooby had been picked up late last night over in Vermont, trying to book a flight to Mexico, and Dale had been snatched off his barstool down at the Nailed Coffin, too drunk to even know what was going on.

"Lot of investigators in both the US and Canada are going to be busy with this one," Chandler mused. "Yvonne and Darius were basically the center of a web. They had over three dozen small-time meth cooks on our side of the border alone, funneling product to their operation in Montreal. More than enough to ignite a turf war with the local gangsters here in Toronto, which led to the nightclub shooting."

"Par for the course. Little guys take all the risks while the fat cats at the top reap all the rewards." Stone growled disgustedly. "And God knows how many innocent people get hurt in the process."

"Speaking of innocent people, how are Lizzy and Holly doing?"

"They've been better but they'll get through it. They're both tough as nails."

"Glad to hear it."

"Thanks for all the help on this."

"You helped me as much as I helped you," Chandler replied. "So next time you decide to jump the border into the Great White North, the first beer's on me. Hell, I'll even take you to a hockey game."

Valentine appeared in the doorway holding a printout.

"I'm from Texas," Stone said. "I don't do hockey."

"We can't all be perfect." Chandler chuckled. "Stay in touch, sheriff. I'll catch you later."

Stone hung up and beckoned to Valentine. "Find anything?"

The young deputy nodded. "Sure did." He handed Stone the sheet of paper. "You were right, sheriff. Just like you suspected, Cynthia Gunther's credit cards were never canceled."

Stone scanned the list of businesses on the printout. Cynthia's card had last been used at a general store in a town called Swallow's Cove, about an hour away.

Stone grabbed his coat. "Hold down the fort," he said to Valentine. "I'm going for a drive."

———

He stopped at the Birch Bark on the way out of town to grab some road food and check up on Holly, who had decided to go to work this morning despite everything that had happened.

Due to the lull between breakfast and lunch, the diner was mostly deserted. Holly was working the counter. She bore a few bruises and a nasty black eye from her battle with Yvonne but she was cheerful and clearly glad to see him.

"There's my knight in shining armor." She grinned. "Or should I say, my knight in a cowboy hat."

"A knight in a cowboy hat just doesn't make any sense," Stone said with a little smile.

She poured him a coffee without being asked. "How are you doing?"

"I'm fine." *Especially for someone who burned a man alive last night in the name of justice,* he thought, but kept it to himself. "How are you and Lizzy holding up?"

"I'm okay but Lizzy's pretty shaken up." Holly poured herself a half-cup of coffee and rested her elbows on the counter, leaning toward him. "She's taking the rest of the week off school." She gave a little shrug. "Who knows, maybe she'll need therapy or something. Lord knows the poor girl's had a rough go of it."

Stone hesitated. "I'm sorry all this happened to you. I kind of feel responsible. Yvonne came after you to get to me."

"Shut up, Luke." Holly smiled when she said it, reaching over to squeeze his hand. "Don't say that. For that matter, don't even *think* it. You moved heaven and hell to get Lizzy back to me. You saved her life, and mine. It's a debt we'll never be able to repay."

"There's no debt," Stone said quietly. "I couldn't stand to lose either one of you."

"The feeling's mutual."

For the next few minutes, they just sat there drinking coffee and looking at each other. They were both comfortable with the silence, knowing that sometimes there is just no need for words.

THIRTY-FOUR

STONE DROVE into Swallow's Cove an hour later.

The small hamlet at the western edge of Garrison County was a popular destination for outdoor enthusiasts. Despite the name, there was no actual cove; instead, the region consisted of a ring of small, well-stocked lakes and thick forests that were home to abundant game. As he steered the Blazer down the main drag, Stone counted three different sporting goods stores.

Spotting his first destination, he pulled into the parking lot of a small general store that boasted no sign to identify the name of the establishment.

The door chimed as Stone walked in. The nameless store was a long, narrow space with cheap shelves crammed full of the usual convenience store supplies. Racks along the wall serviced the town's primary tourist industry with a selection of camouflage clothing and fishing garb. There was even a small display of hunting rifles for sale in a cabinet behind the counter.

The clerk manning the cash register was a middle-aged guy wearing an Aaron Lewis t-shirt and sporting a short-trimmed beard. He looked up from the magazine he was reading as Stone entered.

"Afternoon," the clerk greeted with a smile, stashing away his reading material. "Welcome to Swallow's Cove."

"Thanks." Stone returned the smile and flashed his badge. "Came up from Whisper Falls, working on a case."

"That right?"

Stone nodded. "How's business been?"

The clerk shrugged. "Well, it's pretty much off-season now, sheriff. Can't say we're doing a rip-roaring amount of commerce lately. But enough to keep food on the table and a little left over for the church plate when it gets passed around Sunday morning."

"So not a lot of visitors this time of year?"

"No, sir." The clerk shook his head. "We get lots of folks renting the cottages in the summer and of course hunters in the fall. But now that summer is long gone and hunting season is just about over? We'll pretty much be a ghost town until the snow falls and the cross-country skiers start showing up. And of course, once the lakes freeze over, we'll get the ice fishers."

"I'm looking for somebody," Stone said. "Came through here a few days ago. Used a credit card at this store. Older gentleman. Thin, balding, walks with a limp."

"Yeah, I remember him."

Stone took out his cellphone, pulled up a photo, and showed it to the man. "That him?"

"Yep, sure is." The clerk nodded. "Bought some groceries and a *lot* of liquor."

Sounds about right, Stone thought. Aloud he asked, "You chat with him at all?"

"Little bit. He wasn't much of a talker, but I managed

to drag a short conversation out of him. Said he lost his wife recently and was in town to mourn her."

"Any chance he said where he's staying?"

"Told me his wife owned a cottage here. I know the place, if you want the address."

Stone put away his phone. "That'd be great."

―――――

Standing outside by the Blazer, Stone made a quick call to the station. Valentine answered the phone and Stone gave the deputy his current location and where he was heading. Judging from the clerk's crudely drawn map and verbal descriptions, the cottage was off the beaten path by a wide margin. He wanted someone to know where he was in case things went sideways.

"Got it." Valentine repeated the address. "Want me to send backup? The way Catfish drives, he could be there in thirty minutes."

"No, I've got it," Stone replied. "In this case, I may need my Bible more than my badge."

"Well, in that case, good luck, preacher."

―――――

Stone followed the map, driving the Blazer along the curving backwoods roads outside of Swallow's Cove. He saw some clapboard cottages that looked dreary squatting among the leafless trees, all gray and weatherworn. Others were painted in cheerful colors, bursts of brightness in the stark autumn landscape. Those that dotted any part of the lakeshore had small boathouses with docks attached. Occasionally he caught sight of a canoe or kayak floating in the water.

It was truly a picturesque area. Stone found himself

thinking that maybe he should rent a cottage next summer, bring a fishing pole and a good book, and spend a few days relaxing. Maybe he would invite Holly and Lizzy to join him.

The further out Stone drove, the more frequent the drab and dilapidated cottages became. He turned onto a dirt road in desperate need of repair, the ruts and potholes only slightly shallower than the surrounding lakes. The cottages on this ill-maintained lane didn't just look decrepit—they looked abandoned.

Except one.

Stone pulled in behind the four-wheel-drive pickup truck parked in the crushed-stone driveway, weeds sprouting up between the pebbles. He exited the Blazer and hiked across the lawn, the uncut grass reaching above his knees.

He studied the cottage, which had seen better years. The roof, littered with countless generations of dead pine needles, sagged like a swaybacked horse, as if no longer able to bear the weight of a hundred summers. Paint flaked off the porch railing and more than half the boards were seriously warped. A brick chimney, mortar crumbling from the cracks, poked up into the sky from the back side of the house, a thread of smoke twisting into the sky.

Stone circled the cottage and found a small porch out back. A huddled figure in a heavy flannel bathrobe sat on a rusty lawn chair by the screen door. He had a glass in his hand, a double-barreled shotgun across his lap, and a faraway look in his eyes.

"Hi, Vince."

"Hello, preacher." Vince Gunther did not look at Stone, merely sipped from his glass. A bottle of rye whiskey stood on a small plastic table next him.

Stone stepped up onto the porch. "We've been

worried, Vince." Stone crossed his arms and leaned against the wall. He kept his movements deceptively casual, but made sure to lean with his left shoulder instead of his right in case he had to reach for the Glock holstered on his hip. Though it seemed pretty clear Gunther's darkness was turned inward, not outward, the shotgun was still cause for concern.

"Worried?" Gunther brayed out a bitter laugh and then drained his drink. He immediately poured more rye into his glass. He didn't offer Stone any. "Yeah, I imagine you would worry. That's what you do, right? Fuss an' fidget over your flock. Anyway, I figured sooner or later you'd figure out where I'd run off to. But truth be told, I thought I would have finished what I came here to do by then." He patted the shotgun like it was an old friend.

"Don't say that," Stone said, feeling like a hypocrite given how many times he had thought about eating a bullet after his daughter died. "Don't even think about making a mistake like that."

"It wouldn't be a mistake. Not for me," Gunther said miserably. "Not after I killed my wife."

"Did you mean to kill her?"

"I DON'T KNOW, DAMMIT!"

Gunther's volcanic outburst was out of character. His thunderous words were accompanied by a violent motion that caused the whiskey to slosh over the rim of his glass and onto his lap. He struggled to collect himself, his grief-lined face trembling before collapsing in tears. He wept for a full minute before bringing himself back under control with a deep breath that sounded more like the gasp of a drowning man.

Stone let the silence hang for another minute before quietly asking, "Vince, what happened?"

Gunther heaved out a longsuffering sigh. "Preacher, you have no idea what it was like. Cynthia had become damn near impossible to live with. I mean, we'd been together so long, but the last year or so, the dementia started creeping in, and it turned my sweet Cynthia into a different person. Mean and bitter."

Stone nodded sympathetically.

"We became strangers living in the same house. Most of the time, I didn't even know who she was anymore."

"You could have told me," Stone said. "I would have helped."

"I know, preacher. You're a good man." Gunther nodded as if agreeing with himself. "I kept telling Cynthia that we should talk to you, get some counseling, but she wouldn't listen. Always led to an argument."

"Sorry to hear that."

"Not as sorry as I am." Gunther took a long drink of whiskey and stared out into the trees. "I was at a loss. Talking didn't work, so I resorted to silence instead. We just stopped talking. Then I took to this stuff." He hoisted his glass. "Started going to town every day and tossing back a couple. Just to take the edge of things, ya know? Then a couple became three or four, which became six or seven, which became…well, you get the drift."

"That's a lot of booze, Vince."

"Yeah, that's what Griz started telling me." Gunther laughed bitterly. "You know you've got a drinking problem when even the bartender tells you to cut back."

Stone smiled at that but it was tinged with sadness. He was listening to a man tell the story of how he had lost his way. He had heard similar stories before and they rarely had happy endings.

"Anyway," Gunther continued, "I kept drinking, my mind got fuzzy, and I started forgetting things. Started having blackouts."

Stone felt frustrated that two of his parishioners had been in so much pain and he hadn't known. But he knew all too well that some people just have a hard time asking for help. Still, that didn't stop him from feeling pretty damn useless.

"I started fantasizing about burning the house down. Not with her in it. Just...I don't know." Gunther shook his head. "Like, maybe if we didn't have the house anymore it would bring her back to her senses. Or make it easier for me to put her in a nursing home. I don't know...my thinking was all muddled. I was on those blood pressure pills I told you about and I was drinking a lot."

You still are, thought Stone.

"I've been trying to remember the day of the fire," Gunther continued. "It's kind of fuzzy, but I remember carrying a bottle of lighter fluid in from the garage because I was going to burn some garbage out back. I'd been drinking, of course—no surprise there. Cynthia was taking a nap in the sunroom. I decided to make myself a cup of coffee to sober up a little, so I turned on the stove. When I set the bottle of lighter fluid down, it tipped over and spilled some on the counter."

He paused, staring off into space, the thousand yard stare of the tragic and the broken. He was quiet for so long that Stone finally prompted, "What happened next?"

"I got angry and decided to go out in the barn and have a drink. I always kept a bottle or two out there. I...I just put on my coat and left the house. Never cleaned up the lighter fluid and never turned off the stove." He looked at Stone with bleary, haunted eyes. "But I swear to God, pastor, I didn't do it on purpose. I didn't mean to kill my Cynthia."

"I believe you," Stone said, and it wasn't a lie. He could feel the man's pain, the heartbreaking anguish in his soul.

"I promised to take care of her. Said my vows to love and honor and cherish. And then I burned her alive. God forgive me because I'll never forgive myself."

Rage infused Gunther's voice. He was furious—with himself. Stone felt sorry for the man, struggling in his own private hell.

"Anyway," Gunther said, "I passed out in the barn and when I woke up, the house was burning. You know the rest."

Stone nodded. Yeah, he knew the rest. Cynthia's burned body. The funeral. All of it. So much grief and tragedy.

Gunther stared at him. "You gonna arrest me, sheriff?"

It occurred to Stone that this was the first time Vince Gunther had ever called him anything other than "pastor" or "preacher."

"Let me ask you something, Vince. Do you think you need help?"

Gunther shook his head forcefully. "I don't need help, sheriff. I just need the pain to end. I need it to stop."

"You need what to stop?"

"The world." Gunther drained the rest of his drink in one shot. "I'm done with it. I don't want to go on living. Not without her. Not without my Cynthia. Not after what I done to her. It wouldn't be right, it wouldn't be fair, and it wouldn't be just."

Justice. Stone rolled the word around his mind. It looked different depending on the circumstances. Sometimes justice looked like a prison cell. Sometimes it looked like an eye-for-an-eye. And sometimes it looked like a double-barreled shotgun in the hands of a tired, heartbroken old man.

"I don't want to live anymore, sheriff. I'm all done." Gunther patted the shotgun again. "This here's my one-way ticket to Heaven. I'm going to see Cynthia and apologize to her, face to face. After that…well, if God wants to send me to Hell, I guess it won't be no big deal, 'cause I'm already living in hell down here."

Stone felt a tightness in his chest. He had a decision to make.

Or did he? Was it really his call to make? When you got right down to it, this choice was between Vince Gunther and his God.

Sometimes justice looks like…

"Vince," Stone said quietly. "I'll be back in an hour. If you want, we can talk more then."

Gunther gave him a long, meaningful look, then toasted him with the empty glass and said, "Goodbye, preacher. Thanks for everything."

Stone walked away and didn't look back.

Not even when the shotgun roared.

THIRTY-FIVE

STONE STOOD IN THE CEMETERY, staring down at the fresh graves.

Luisa Valdez's service had been well-attended. Vince Gunther's had not. Stone could barely remember what he said at either one.

The late afternoon air was cold. The forecast called for snow tomorrow. The dark, fresh dirt would be covered in virgin white. Stone clamped his Stetson down tighter and buttoned up his ranch coat as a sharp breeze cut through the gravestones. Save for the brisk, biting wind, it was quiet. With less than an hour of daylight left, he considered staying here until dusk settled its shadows across the dead.

He heard footsteps behind him, followed by a soft voice.

"Luke?"

He turned to see Lizzy standing there. "Hey, Liz," he said. "How are you?"

"I'm okay. Went back to school today." She came over and stood beside him, looking down at Luisa's grave. "I miss her," she said quietly.

"She was your friend," Stone said. "You'll always miss her."

"I can't stop thinking about it." Lizzy reached up and brushed away a tear sneaking down her cheek. "Her death, I mean. It just seems so...I dunno...pointless."

"It was," Stone replied. "There was absolutely no reason she had to die."

Lizzy pulled her coat more tightly around herself. "There's real evil in this world, isn't there?" She didn't really phrase it as a question. "People who hurt other people just because they want to. People who kill just because they can."

Stone reflected on some of the wicked men and women he had fought during his warrior days. The terrorists, the drug cartels, the sex traffickers, the murderous tyrants. So much sin, so much sickness, so much evil. "Yeah, the world is full of people like that."

"Yeah, well, maybe God should just kill them all," Lizzy said heatedly. "Then the rest of us wouldn't have to suffer."

"Sometimes He does, Lizzy. But only sometimes." Stone put a hand on her shoulder. "Don't let the injustice of the world turn your heart cold."

"Kind of hard when your friend is in a coffin."

"The people who killed Luisa are dead. There must be some comfort in that, right?"

"Sure." Lizzy shrugged. "Just not as much as you might think."

———

A few hours later, Holly and Luke sat on his back deck, enjoying a fire and drinks. They sat in separate chairs but close enough that their arms, elbows, and hands occasionally touched. It was enough—for now—for both of them.

Stone stared into the dancing flames as off in the darkness coy-wolves howled, the mournful cry of the hunter. Lying beside him, Max's ears pricked up at the sound. But he quickly relaxed, having grown accustomed to the frequent night-song of the four-legged predators that roamed the mountains.

Holly sipped from her glass of white wine and looked at Stone. "Pretty serious over there, cowboy. Penny for your thoughts?"

"Just thinking about darkness and light," Stone replied softly. "How there's too much of the first and not enough of the second."

"That's pretty cynical for a preacher."

"Maybe, but it's the truth. Too much evil, not enough justice."

Stone felt his own cold darkness coiled deep within him. He had unleashed it last winter on the child-killing survivalists and then summoned it again to deal fiery justice to Darius Cole. Was it right? Not in the eyes of the law. But what about in the eyes of God?

Stone silently admitted that sometimes his vigilante executions felt divinely sanctioned, blessed from above. But other times, in the aftermath of those kills, he felt like he had played right into the hands of the devil himself.

But he also knew he would kill again. Sometimes justice demanded it.

He shifted in his chair so that his shoulder was pressed against Holly. She turned his head and smiled warmly as he raised his glass of Jack & Coke, lots of ice, easy on the Jack.

"To justice," he said.

Holly tapped her glass against his. "I'll drink to that.

A LOOK AT BOOK THREE:
KILLING CREED

Lucas Stone, full-time sheriff, part-time preacher, and sometimes-vigilante, stumbles into a war between local truckers and a biker gang. The rural highways of Garrison County have become road-raging kill zones and the corpses are starting to stack up like cordwood.

Pulling the strings is The Remnant, an army of neo-Nazi terrorists. When the feds get involved, Stone finds himself playing second fiddle to Tanya Bester, an FBI supervisor with a chip on her shoulder and a mile-wide competitive streak. Not content to just take over his investigation, Bester invades Stone's personal life as well.

The battle between the truckers and bikers is just a warmup for a wider war. The Remnant is determined to make a lethal power play against a government they deem weak and corrupt. When Stone stands in their way, they set their crosshairs on Whisper Falls, targeting law dogs and laymen with impunity.

The Remnant believe they are a ruthless, irresistible force. But they are about to slam against Stone's cold, immoveable belief in primal justice.

AVAILABLE MARCH 2023

ABOUT THE AUTHOR

Mark Allen was raised by an ancient clan of ruthless ninjas and now that he has revealed this dark secret, he will most likely be dead by tomorrow for breaking the sacred oath of silence. The ninjas take this stuff very seriously.

When not practicing his shuriken-throwing techniques or browsing flea markets for a new katana, Mark writes action fiction. He prefers his pose to pack a punch, likes his heroes to sport twin Micro-Uzis a la Chuck Norris in Invasion USA, and firmly believes there is no such thing as too many headshots in a novel.

He started writing "guns 'n' guts" (his term for the action genre) at the not-so-tender age of 16 and soon won his first regional short story contest. His debut action novel, The Assassin's Prayer, was optioned by Showtime for a direct-to-cable movie. When that didn't pan out, he published the book on Amazon to great success, moving over 10,000 copies in its first year, thanks to its visceral combination of raw, redemptive drama mixed with unflinching violence.

Now, as part of the Wolfpack team, Mark Allen looks forward to bringing his bloody brand of gun-slinging, bullet-blasting mayhem to the action-reading masses.

Mark currently resides in the Adirondack Mountains of upstate New York with a wife who doubts his ninja skills because he's always slicing his fingers while chopping veggies, two daughters who refuse to take tae kwon do, let alone ninjitsu, and enough firepower to ensure that he is never bothered by door-to-door salesmen.